From Labor to Letters

Address:
Bilingual Press
Hispanic Research Center
Arizona State University
P.O. Box 872702
Tempe, Arizona 85287-2702
(602) 965-3867

From Labor to Letters

A Novel Autobiography

Miguel Méndez

Translated from the Spanish
by David William Foster

Bilingual Press/Editorial Bilingüe

Tempe, Arizona

ISBN 0-927534-70-3 (cloth)
Published simultaneously in a softcover edition. ISBN 0-927534-66-5

Library of Congress Cataloging-in-Publication Data

Méndez M., Miguel.
[Entre letras y ladrillos. English]
From labor to letters : a novel autobiography / Miguel Méndez ; translated from the Spanish by David William Foster.
p. cm.
ISBN 0-927534-70-3 (cloth). – ISBN 0-927534-66-5 (pbk.)
1. Méndez M., Miguel. I. Foster, David William. II. Title.
PQ7079.2.M46E5813 1997
863–dc21 97-3271
CIP

PRINTED IN THE UNITED STATES OF AMERICA

Cover design by Bidlack Creative Services

Back cover photo by Ray Manley Portraits

Acknowledgments

Partial funding provided by the Arizona Commission on the Arts through appropriations from the Arizona State Legislature and grants from the National Endowment for the Arts.

[redacted]

Reflections

I believe I could write several autobiographies, each one different but all essentially the same. There are so many isolated facts that end up on the fringes of our summations. This is, perhaps, because real or willed forgetfulness has shrouded them in mist as the result of our passing through the space of the spheres, whose time appears to be infinite. Certainly it is immeasurable. Moreover, an autobiography in the form of a novel is just that: a novel whose framework, background and general outlines are to be found in a network of anecdotes and sayings that suggest the character and the life of the autobiographer who is telling his own story. Thus, strange motifs and events parade across the page behind ramparts of letters, events that are fabled, events that are sad, if they are not filled with the humor and irony that envelop like a shell the vision of raw reality. The numerous anecdotes and episodes to be found in a life full of convergences and circumstances are determined by the marked influence of settings and microcosms that generate the most extraordinary appearances, constant incubators of things unheard of and sublime, in a "going" rather than a becoming, one that is alternately fortunate and bitter and more than often chaotic, the result of any one of a number of passions that constantly besiege and constrain us. Nevertheless, life inspires me to laughter. My fellow men are oh so very silly, and I am the only one among them who is a clown devoid of anything funny. Yet . . . when I cry on the inside like a lonely child, I hide among the mirrors so I won't feel sad. That's when I really laugh out loud.

From the position of my two universes, the tangible one and the ideal one, I know I have skimmed over seas clouded by unknown and familiar voices, seas that are at the same time filled with an endless range of faces of the living and the dead, with the air of spectral dimensions of ages and places now lost in the distance.

Now then, soul brothers, let me be honest with you like a son of Sonora: I say to you in complete confidence and with feeling that this first autobiographical novel was dictated to me by an I that has only recently begun to glow with the golden outlines of an intense nostalgia.

No one is forced or implored, reader, to be present here. If you are willing to witness this wordiness which overflows the channels and avenues of *From Labor to Letters,* I bid you enter. If it is not to your liking to venture forth in a cosmos other than your own, well, may God bless you and protect us both.

From Labor to Letters

I came into the world like a little angel passing through on my way to any station whatever. But there are sudden turns in life, ones that are completely unexpected. My mother gave birth to me in the seventh month. The doctors in the hospital in the small mining town considered my case to be totally without hope: my intestines were minimal and nonfunctioning, and my inner organs were all jumbled together, not to mention my other organs, which were half-developed or already waning. Such was the case that the doctor in charge of my care spoke frankly to my parents. It was in the afternoon, the mountains filled with copper, perforated by artificial caverns, moments before the sun would yield to the stars. My mother told me about it, always beset by my questions. Take this child home. He won't live out the night. It was a miracle that I'd lived for three or four weeks, because I couldn't even urinate. I don't know how I came to have any of the veins necessary for the blood to flow, not to mention that apparatus that pumps it. In that humble miner's house, the dying baby brought his family and his parents' friends together. I have always been borderline, and not just on the border between two countries. I certainly was on the border there, between life and death, barely having come forth into the light from the maternal cloister. Nobody shed a tear, but more than one person had damp eyes for my parents' suffering. At least, I would be off to a better place without having sinned. The patroness of sadness, Our Lady of Tears, was not the only one keeping vigil that night. She who cuts the thread of time and erases space waited patiently in the doorway, covered by a shawl woven from the thread of day and night. But—blessed be the "buts"—the unknown horseman also arrived, that great lord, Sir Mystery.

Doña Chuy López, an older light-complexioned woman, approached my mother, her arms cradled. Put your son here, María. I will cure him. My mother was reluctant to give me up, and she covered my chest, fearful. No way in the world would she let go of me. She was determined to keep my soul from escaping from my weak cage. Let me have him, woman. I won't harm him. Our family legend says that Doña Chuy spoke to me with great tenderness. She turned her gaze upward and spoke to God with a soft murmur, giving me drops from her own harvest, barely rubbing me with her hands, her voice and her movements exuding tenderness. By dawn I was crying relatively energetically. I gained in strength week after week. I was going to live. Doña Chuy López had cured me. She always insisted on denying it. God cured him, she would say. All I did was to say to the Lord, Lord give this bit of flesh strength. See how he's hanging on. Help him, for he's making an effort on his own. Before the year was out, my body was overflowing with health and life. I think the crisis of gaining strength miraculously had the result of making me hungry to live, almost insatiable. When I started to read at the age of five, the boundless appetite of my jumbled innards was joined by the imperative to feed my intellect. From that time on, I devoured literature.

Here I am now, seated at my office desk, located in this Spanish Department at the University of Arizona. At the same time that I look at my students' papers and go over the assignments for the course I am teaching, I think of other times and write and write. After these reminiscences about the days immediately following my birth, recollections about other twists in my life come unbidden to mind, ones that turned my destiny in unimagined directions.

I suddenly went from a small communal village in Sonora to living in a city in the United States. I quickly exchanged a small family setting conditioned by voices in Spanish for a chorus of strange notes in the English language. I passed overnight from the protection of the hearth to complete defenselessness. Installed in adolescence, in the antechamber of youth, still a neighbor to childhood, I became a construction worker during eight months of the year and a day laborer in the fields for the other four. My character and experience as a wage earner was migratory in both cases. The age of fourteen was the border where, alternating childlike puberty and deep-voiced youth, I forged my spirit for undertaking a struggle that would be as tough and lasting as the most unpredictable of wars. Before I even reached the age of fifteen, with my pubic region already in full feather and with the metamorphosis that leads from the early stages to the realm of full manhood, I met my first lover. This was a change that was more gentle than it was brusque, with smiling vigils and verses written to the stars.

The other turn, wrenching in the extreme as far as the inconceivable is concerned, happened to me at the age of forty. Although I had never spent a single day in an American classroom and my only official education consisted of six years in grade school in El Claro, Sonora, Mexico, I became a university professor. This happened on the first Monday of September 1970. Three days before, on the last Friday of the month of August, I had divorced myself forever from my employment in the humblest forms of hard labor to wed myself to the tasks of the highest academic level. My life underwent, then, such a transformation that I suddenly found myself caught between bewilderment and euphoria.

My eyes are heavy and I need to doze a bit if I can, an owl's nap

That day there were only three of us snotty brats in action, barefoot, with feet more or less like that of wild billygoats. We must have been about eight or nine years old, shirts flapping in shreds in the wind, although I was naked from the waist up, our pants stiff with sweat, dust, and pee, with yellow stains on the inside from our shit. We were hunting rattlesnakes for my brother Mario to behead by snapping them like a whip. All of the sudden we spied from the hills next to the houses a group of five horses and their accompanying knock-kneed riders. Old Don Palomo was riding in front, his hands tied behind his back. Five members of the communal farm who were acting as policemen were leading Santana. We flung ourselves downhill, racing as fast as we could, our feet sending rocks flying and smashing the jutting grass. Our luck would have it that they came to a halt under a large mesquite. Get the hell out of here, you bunch of blabbing kids, sons of bitches, this here is none of your business. Old Fart, a shitty pistol stuck under a belt, makes any dimwit think he's Pancho Villa. We ignored him and his doubled rope. They called him Trots and he was useless even for poisoning dogs, which is why they'd made him up as a "representative of justice, damn it." Old man Palomo's hair, face, shirt, and hands were covered with dried blood and continued oozing fresh blood. Tarungas Ruiz, gang leader, asked me to get some water for the prisoner. Go on, Mayco, run get some water for this old fart. His smacker's drier than Delgadina's cute one. I went inside the house and grabbed a cup, filling it with water. How come you're in such a hurry. I'm taking a cup of water to old man Palomo. They've got him out there covered with blood. He drank half the water, and Tarungas poured the rest over his head, which washed about half the blood off his face. I didn't even see my mother come out. You're sure a bunch of lowly cowards. What did that poor defenseless man do to you. Go back in your house, lady, and don't go sticking your nose in things that are none of your business. Shut up, Trots. Look, Doña María, this old man's lady is out like a light, turned into a sandwich with red chile sauce. This time this sweet little dove went too far. And you can be sure this time his wife's not going to be able to tell about it. In my opinion, she won't mend herself anymore, and nobody will put her back together like before. The neighbors threw stones to get this one to drop the stick and get the devil out of him. So, what else, but now we're taking him off to jail.

Don Palomo had married Ramononga five years before. She was barely twenty-five, but she had a humpback that went with her camel's hump of a nose. The man had shown up from some far-off village. There was not a tooth left in his mouth, just like one of those small drawstring pouches of tobacco. Folks like to gossip, and they claimed that he was on the run from some stabbings attributed to him. Don Palomo's best line of defense against this sort of talk was his choirboy face. He lovey-dovey'd Ramononga up, the first boyfriend the poor gimp had ever had. She said yes to the guy with yellowish chicken eyes, but on condition he eat a loaf of sugar in public. To the tune of the laughter and taunts of the crowd and with midday defeated under the weight of the afternoon sun, the old lover set about to do away with the block of sugarcane candy, hard as ironwood. It took him some time, and although he bled and slobbered, his eyes filled with tears, that stubborn old coot got it all down. He made a life with the hunchback for a period of five years filled with squabbles, shovings, insults of all sorts, and barkings. The first time he got it into his head to give Ramononga a serenade of kicks and slaps, things backfired on the old grump. Ramononga, used to chopping wood, lifting sacks of grain, milking cows, and doing all sorts of heavy work, was as strong as a first-class mule. When she set about slugging it out, she could hit with all the force of a pipe with just her hands, like any lady macho. She left the old man out of his wits and with his mouth hanging open. A swarm of avid-mouthed flies sucked away at their leisure at his bloodied snot. Ramononga delivered a total of four kids, each one uglier than bad luck itself. When the old man packed her off to St. Peter, clubbed to a pulp, she was carrying a fetus several weeks old.

During the present 1993-1994 academic year, I will celebrate twenty-five years in the classroom, as well as the same number of years devoting myself to this sort of scribbling and carting my manuscripts off to the publisher and, thanks to the magic of printing, seeing them turned into books whose contents are novels, short stories, and the like. It's been forty-eight years divided among experiences as different as breaking my back in "common" jobs, as Don Vasconcelos would say, and in teaching courses in Spanish language and literature. Added to the foregoing stretch, my first fourteen years as a Sonoran peasant, along with any number of intervening adventures, prepare me—and indeed impel me—peremptorily to write a procession of reminiscences about some of the facts gleaned from this heavy wake of memories. They are tenacious memories that cling with claws to the retinas of my melancholy. How many memories there must be that serve as paths for my nostalgia begging to be fed, go and fetch the past in the realm it inhabits, and bring it back to me alive, putting it on the exact plane where perennial time and space reside.

My new situation, as calm as it was, did not free me at the time, nor in the intervening years across the decades, from a longing for those days of bitter struggle, which after all corresponded to the flowering of my youth. My world, my companions in the struggle, my neighborhood with its face of poverty are suddenly frozen by absence and distance. Our steps and the paths we follow go in entirely opposite directions, but the memories remain united, intact.

The flow of anecdotes and so many unexpected events, drenched in sweat, blood, fear, laughter, as spontaneous and fleeting as befits casual happenings, have jumbled together. Over it all there floats the specter of an outburst, the echo that fizzles out and grows distant like a vacant scenario. In these my new spaces, no matter how many multiple voices there are, everything is silence. An ivory tower shines brightly in every head, or maybe it's one of lime-painted bricks. Every step is programmed, redeemed by guides and syllabi. Classroom voices are currents subordinated to heavy doors and clocks. The teacher, a disciplined jailer, contemplates himself. He has at hand a pair of scissors with chronometrical blades. Here life and letters are analyzed in a contemplative trance. I'm used to forging whirlpools for myself on this trained river in which I turn and turn like a spring in reverse that places me in one piece in moments in the past, each one distant in terms of both time and place from the others. This game gives me pleasure. It's a miracle! This combined task seems right to me and makes me feel good. It jumps from a bookish setting to those realms that favored my chancy life, devoid of situations guided by a priori scripts.

I have over the years resigned myself to this situation of a teacher and writer with very much of a sedentary existence. This is what I really like now. My mind, however, has taken on a dynamic that at least for the time being gives me no peace. It exhorts me in a demanding way and precipitates in me a stampede of memories and speculative considerations of the most disparate sort. It likewise undertakes to lead me to thoughts that are weakly shaded with an impoverished logic, one all the more questionable for being of my own making.

I've developed a stubborn and annoying fever with respect to bygone days. It gets worse at night, quite a bit worse. Loli insists I rest. She claims I'm exhausted. It makes me laugh. How can these tasks of a well-cushioned man tire me out? So, I chat with Miguelito and Isabelilla about the time when under the pounding sun at three in the afternoon in the month of June, here in the desert, with a heat wave that sent the mercury up to forty-five degrees and me engaged in moving superheavy materials "of the kind that make machos give birth," the boss came up to me, looked at me funny, furrowed his brow and observed: Hey, you don't look as dark as the others, you're all red even up to your eye balls, do you feel all fucked out?, you're chitchatting like a rattle and walking like a drunk. What's with you, anyway? No, nothing at all. It's just that I've got a triple-grade fever. He felt my forehead with astonishment. Sonofamother! You're as hot as a tortilla griddle. I'm going to run you home; you can die there any way you want. But there was no way he could convince me. A half hour later, with our eight-hour shift over, we hopped aboard Indian Encinas's rattletrap of a truck. Since we were working far from town, several of us took turns driving. OK men, let's stop here at the Chinamen's store and get ourselves a few beers. Even though I've never liked to drink, there I was tagging along behind. I bought myself three ice-cold large cans. During the half-hour drive back I drank one after the other, so there wasn't a drop left in any of the cans. It was like I was on fire. I took a swallow and my insides sounded like I was putting a fire out, and why not, because the liquid was falling on my innards, which were like a single burning pit. Two of my buddies helped me climb down. They as much as carried me into the hovel where I lived. They dropped me on the bed like a sack of stones. But first they shoved some books aside, some open, some shut, to make room for me. From far away I heard Indian Encinas making some remarks. Fucking Miguel, sure he's real drunk. Fatty Romero was checking the books out and making a big effort to read some words out loud. Get a load of this guy, brother, as if he knew how to read. Pour it on man! Lots of fucking books all over the place. Cri-cri-critique of purr pour pure reason fucking shit of this nerd, hey, let's vamos, you just stay bro! The next day I stumbled in to work, my head still roaring, but I didn't crack. So now, with an office with all the comfort in the world and I'm going to stay home, sure what else, and pamper myself just like I was a baby! Give me a break. You just refuse to get it, don't you, pal, even if you really do understand. Back then you were young, barely twenty years old, and now you've turned sixty-three. Well that's just why I'm stronger and younger, pure accumulated youth, I'm four times a fifteen-year-old and the shrub's still bearing fruit. My children shake their heads, Loli just stares at me and I'm pleased as punch with myself.

So, let's see how fucking good you guys are at riding wild calves, because us, we've got real balls. Don't swerve to the side, Huilo, damn it, let's see who gets dragged the farthest, those calves really get to me. Anyone who gives up is a crappy hog's behind. We ride up into the hills with two ropes we "borrow" for a while. There are six of us altogether, each one as sweaty and cramped as the other. All the time we are half shouting at each other, in a single raucous display that not even birds with their early singing would equal. The sun isn't out yet and we're already moving fast. Well, here, your parents are really foul mouthed, thousands of bad words; nothing to do though, that's the way it is. In my house no one uses cuss words, but I do, with my buddies. By ten anyone is talking like the big kids or like the cowboys and the drunks. Marquitos Moreno, Mole, and Cucochón, who all live on top of each other, over there toward the edge of the communal farm on the road to Trincheras, dropped by for a visit. Every time we get together, we go for each other's throat; that's our way to say good-bye, or else, something happens. Marquitos's dad was hauled off to jail yesterday in Santana for having said that the communal farm bank had stolen his entire wheat harvest. He showed up drunk and yelled at them that they were a bunch of thieving sons of bitches. When Cucochón is afraid he starts making all kinds of faces.

He's starting to wrinkle his brow already. Everybody agreed to let him ride the first animal. Huilo had picked for the lead animal, a real mean calf more than a year old. Since it's one of those like zebus, with a humped back, we were all a bit freaked out, and say no more. He lassoed it and brought it to a sudden halt. We all pulled together to get its head against a paloverde. But it sure was a goddamned mean-spirited bull, and you could see the red rage in its eyes. Mole smacked him on the nose. This'll get your attention and make you act like a man, you SOB. OK, Cuchochón, come on, guests first. Cuchochón hops on, wailing scandalously. You guys sure are bad. You want me to die (sob sob sob). I came to see you like a friend and now you want to kill me. Shit! You guys from the lowlands sure are cowards. No, this one ends up a sissy faster than you think. Watch your mouth, Huilito, you little squirt, you're wrong; I'll mount that mean little bull. Just so you know, you bastards, I've got real hair down here, and I'm already starting to milk it. OK, let's go. We got a rope around the calf so the rider could grip the animal's slippery back with his hands and knees, and we were all set to enjoy the spectacle of Marquitos Moreno, the lowlands cowboy. Once he was up on the back of the animal, Marquitos no longer sounded like himself, but he talked like his father. Hold on a moment, you SOBs, if you bastards don't pay attention and respect me, then your mother can go get another hole in her behind. As soon as this bull tries to rear, I'm going to shout Viva Almazán! and you guys shout Viva! too. If you don't shout Viva! I'll beat you purple with my fists. OK, let the animal go, you big asses! So we let go of the bull's halter, and that bugger starts bucking on the stony path and then sets off among the spiny cactuses. The monster rears up high, and Marquitos flies off like the sky belongs to him. To hell with Almazán. He lets out the most terrified cry in the world: Help, sweet mama! We pick up as best we can, from among the sharp rocks and the daggerlike chollas, what's left of the candidate Almazán's supporter. He's bleeding all over the place. We carry his battered body over to the shade of an ironwood. Deep moanings come from his knees, his trunk, his spine, and his head. This fucker is gonna die, all of him. Don't say it Arnulfo, shut up, don't even say it. What are we going to do to make him better, because if we don't we'll get the belt for sure. We got to go get some water to wash his face and see if we can snitch some aspirins. But we're right next to the cemetery. Shit, if Marquitos dies on us, he's home, so to speak. We carried everything we could to Marquitos, even a bottle of chicken broth Arnulfo snuck out of his house. Later that afternoon, about eight hours after being thrown, Marquitos got up, his legs like they were made of jelly and his eyes going every which way. He took some steps like a newborn billygoat. We set off on foot as best we could. The three of us whose houses were nearby got home OK. The three of them, with the battered Marquitos in the middle, had a long trek ahead of them. We learned that the feathered cowboy did not die, because later we never heard anything about him.

Once we got to be ten, there was nothing that could kill us off. By that time we were safe from murderous things. How could there be anything left to do us in. We'd survived the measles, scarlet fever, chickenpox, whooping cough, and falling out of trees. What with so many spiny pricks from cactus, tetanus could give us only heaves and high fevers. From so many wounds and accidents and all sorts of aches and pains, we had ended up with a supertough hide that was death resistant. At night, if you could see us sleeping, you'd have mistaken us for sure for real children.

I congratulate myself on being a solemnly ignorant, simple, and foolish man. I've never been able to have anything to do with people who know how to gauge time, take symmetrical and telescopic measurements, and other crazy things involving a lot of numbers, laboratories, and philosophical treatises. Everything that looks like logic makes me die laughing.

In any case, an author ought to have his own ideas about time, even if no one else shares them. In this way, he has an anchor for his works and can give them a solid structure. So if I'm meditating now about things having to do with time as a concept, it's because I have a real need for a thesis that will underpin and secure my literary work. But in any case, whether I'm boring or if I'm entertaining, I say what anyone can say: it's all the same—my bones rattle, rain or shine.

As far as I'm concerned, time in itself is not only something that's a matter of a localized, partial conception, but something that's universal, indivisible, just like space. This thing about parceling out and setting up boundaries to define both concepts in a conclusive way is the whim of a terrestrial order, and one that's artificial as a consequence. We human beings are phenomena that are integrated locally and temporally as mere reflexes of a perennial timespace and manifested as material figures. We are ephemeral beings of a planetarytimespace sort. Seen from the angle of another galaxy, this concept would be equivalent to life, in so far as the latter, so fleeting, is revealed in a physical form.

I am ensconced in my office, and as if I didn't have anything else to keep my mind busy, it occurs to me to reflect on these and other matters. My labyrinthine lucubration's make me laugh out loud. If someone ends up reading this and doesn't understand it while understanding it, he should know that he's in agreement with the same person who has written on the interstellar air.

Every intellectual has a rhythm whose essence serves to integrate his thinking being with an a priori infinite and unique cosmos. Nevertheless, "each person is a world unto himself." Or to put it differently, every individual universe works also in accord with a specific code. In the case of my code, I'm certain that from even before I was born it was full of atavistic elements that are genealogical and extremely complex, which I have had to fight continually. Someone once expressed the opinion that if you don't know something, you discover it rather than learn it. I'm a habitual explorer, always discovering continents that have already been discovered. As far as diving into the daily sea for real pearls, the only ones I find are lacking in any brilliance. Nevertheless, I am consoled by the childish idea that these uncultured stones glow with the chimerical enthusiasm emanating from my illusions. I smile, confident that by a miracle some reader—since there is no such thing as an orphan book—will bless these written words with the light of his eyes, so that they will mirror that light.

If I ever was a vagrant painting tracks on dusty trails, I'm mentally speaking even more of one now, as I retrace ethereal topographies of my cosmos, there in those realms where the mysteries reside, the ones that correspond to me. I, the one who is eternally ignorant and identified with some ciphers and a name, do not know who I am. As a consequence, I delve around in the innards of what I once was, searching for something that will define me as to whether I will proceed forward toward the future, or maybe I'll advance backwards, in a circle, to stumble over the very instant prior to my birth. Can you go forward into the future following a path back into the past? Ah! Tangible being and the present moment are both the infinite synthesis of the universal timespace. Yet I still don't know who I am, and here I am smiling, filled with pleasure. I am still a mischievous child, only now I no longer take watches apart and lose the main spring. Rather, I ruin ideas and cast their pieces to the wind like so many drops of color, so that time and space will swallow them up as though they were happily volatile confetti.

What is strange about these nights filled with fever and dreams that intrude without asking me what I think about them is that I repeatedly turn over the same obsessions. I see myself among a hundred workmen climbing all over the skeletons of buildings under construction in Phoenix in 1953. I see over and over again so clearly the faces of my comrades in arms, despite the fact that forty years have gone by since then. Images, things the way they were, and anecdotes appear to me in such sharp outlines. They come to me repeatedly all in a jumble. Then there's the essay on the life and death of languages that Professor Evans asked me for. I don't especially like that sort of writing because it requires a world of research. I am not a scholar. I invent situations rather than memorize them. If there's something I don't know, I pull it out of my sleeve, without having to knock my brains out in the process. On top of it all is the chronicle in verse about the time Camilo José Cela stayed with us here in Tucson. He came as a guest so I could show him the places described in my novel *El sueño de Santa María de las Piedras*. He's a genial old sport and we spent two weeks wandering from town to town and from one scenic point to the other, always with a notebook and pencil in hand. He jotted material down that he would use as a filler in his novel *Cristo versus Arizona*. Then this rush of reminiscences about my childhood and my precocious acts of barbarism. Since I don't have any room left to store up stories, I let them burst forth, and then I cast a spell on them in the form of literature so they won't go on trying my patience. Tomorrow is Friday. I will devote the end of the week exclusively to the fever. Monday I'll be as fresh as a daisy, just like when Loli puts potato slices on my forehead.

How pretty God is. All of these fields are for my recreation. This is my Land, this large ball. I contemplate it in the sun when it rises round and full. I also see my planet reflected in the moon of the moon. In every star I know it is there. In the morning I usually climb one of my hills, the highest one my feet can attain. I am filled with happiness by the climb. Ouch, I stepped on a thorn. I pull it out, and a large red drop forms and loses shape as it drips. I hurriedly urinate on the pricked spot. It hurts deeply. As soon as I can find some fresh cow dung, I'll smear the wound and that will take care of it. How the horizon stretches out before me. I can make out an enormous circumference, with me in the middle, the bellybutton of the world. I look up at the sky, and it looks down on me. My soul is filled with jubilant laughter.

Now I start down toward my house. The rattles of a snake, partially spiraled, partially a jab of lightening, greet me with their autochthonous music. If Mario had come along with me, he'd be whirling it like a propeller of a motor. I would beg Mario, cousin, spare its life. Then he would throw the ropelike body that slithers and rears up like a vortex down toward the cushion of bushes in the gully.

Nothing will ever change now, never ever. I will always and eternally be a child. My parents will be beside me, my brothers, my relatives, my friends, and all of this will serve for me to exist. This earth wrapped in flames and blowing dust, covered with thorns, with sunsets and shadowy faces, all of this is what I long for. What do I care about the vast, naked badlands, the dunes and the infinite sands. I know how to dream, and I will blanket them with literature, with so many drawings and colors that they will surprise and provoke envy in the very forests of legend.

I am seated here with my back against the trunk of my house's mesquite. My mother appears and smiles at me. She sees me deep in thought, lost in that realm where the spoken word is banned.

She knows me and does not interrupt me with questions. Before when they used to ask me about my states of meditation and profound isolation, I would just shrug my shoulders. What is there for me to know. . . .

I agreed to have a cup of coffee and chat with Jeremiah here at the university, in one of the places in the Student Union. Whenever I have a talk with Jeremiah I end up laughing at his silly ideas and my own too. He has gotten it into his head that he is one of the world's great inventors. It's the same thing with me, with this idea that I am a writer and that language is so much putty in my hands. Jeremiah is Mexican by background and a professor of English with a doctorate and everything. He manages to get some Spanish out with the help of Gringo words here and there. I see myself in Jeremiah's wild nuttiness as though it were a carnival mirror. He will go down in history as a revolutionizing inventor, and he says so without blushing in the least. Suffering from the same delusion, I will pass into posterity as a real author, as a pioneer of border writing. Yes, no doubt about it, I go from storm to storm, from sunny day to sunny day, filling pages with writing, except when I sketch texts out in my head. There is only one small detail standing between illusion and greatness: I'm not Gimpy Cervantes and I'm not Unamuno the Owl. Of course, no one can take the Miguel away from me. OK, Jeremiah, how many dogs are there on the scaffold. Here are the blueprints for an invention that'll make me a millionaire for sure. Just take a look at these drawings. This project is called "The dancing buoys." Look here, these balls will be in the water, about a mile from the beach. Inside each ball, are you paying attention?, there'll be ballast so they won't rock, you know. Now a wave'll come down like a bat out of hell, see, and wham!, it'll knock them toward the beach. But the ballast will make them rock back, and once again the waves'll come in night and day, and they'll be like rocking and rolling, on and on, without stopping a single second. Ay Chihuahua, Jeremiah, you've gone and invented perpetual motion. No, really, your invention is great. Don't make fun of me, you dope of a writer. The sea's the one with perpetual motion, and that's exactly why you've got to harness it, because it's just like a round river, get it? You've got to put down millions of dancing buoys, and with the drop of electricity each one generates, we can light any city on the coast. He unfurled a design with lines on the table, and it gave him license to go ahead and let loose with a flood of highly exotic technical terms, which ironically is the only thing he's capable of inventing. Then, during a number of minutes that neither he the inventor nor I can count, each of us falls into his own satirical game of chimeras. He went on talking to himself about his invention, and I fell into the past spaces of my childhood with fleeting flashes of when I was in my twenties. Fantasy and fever usually go hand in hand. Jeremiah and I circle like two planets in orbit but around different suns. Suddenly I float to the surface of my self-absorption. Jeremiah is going on and on, full of enthusiasm, and in his right hand he's clutching a small aluminum sphere. It's a miniature model of his dancing buoy. It turns out to be one of those floats used to regulate the water in the tank of a toilet. I glance at my watch and dash off to my class on the Novel of the Revolution. Hey, don't leave. Take a look at this little thing. You'll be my partner, and for just five thousand bucks you'll make millions, millions. . . .

We're finishing up *The Underdogs*. After Azuela, we'll do Martín Luis Guzmán. We did a bit of *Ulises criollo*. Right now we're on Nellie Campobello. After that, we'll read *El resplandor* and one of Rafael Muñoz's books. OK, that's that. When the class is over, I leave for home, take an aspirin, jump into bed and ask Loli to make me some chicken soup. She makes me some nice tacos with meat, and that's that. It makes no difference whether I'm sick or not, I never lose my appetite.

Yes, that's right, students, Nellie Campobello's power of perception and synthesis is something unique. Her two short books, *Las manos de mamá* and *Cartucho* are more than enough to guarantee her a secure place in Mexican literary history. Her place is unquestionable, and at the most some fool could try to ignore her. But, Professor Méndez, her name and her works are rarely cited. Well, that's because she published so little. But then look at Rulfo. Why is she ignored, since it's not a matter of marketplace competition.

Maybe she's overlooked out of envy, because she's from the north, or maybe because she's a woman. For a lot of mediocre minds neither old age nor death is enough to excuse talent. Let's continue. Her brief narratives are so vivid in their masterful elaboration, and she always pays close attention to the authenticity of the themes that provide the source for the stories she has to tell, whether she herself witnessed them or whether they were told to her in commentaries or conversations. The setting of a northern village in the midst of the revolution is elaborated from every angle. She is just as subjective when dealing with flying bullets as she is in dealing with inner feelings. Her stories, her sketches, her narratives, however you want to call them, engage our attention and draw out our feelings. Even if she is recreating tragedy and toughness, the spirit of an artist, of a sensitive young girl, of a beautiful woman, comes through in her prose. What an extraordinary talent that woman had. Even if her work is classified as part of the Novel of the Revolution, it is quite unique and worthy of universal attention. OK, students, take another look at *Cartucho* this weekend and bring me an essay on what we've read and discussed. Fili, the cut-up in the group, asked me if Campobello would have read Borges. I don't know, Fili, except that both dealt in a profound manner with human essence. Professor Méndez, do you plan on being as good as writers with laurels and fame? Pipe down, Fili, don't start in with your nonsense. Don't make fun of contraband. If I don't measure up, at least I have a name. Anyway I'll tell you later after the crazy bony lady carries me away. The other students laugh and I force myself to join in. Did you ever meet that genius Borges? Yes, I met him and we exchanged a few words. What impression did the Argentine make on you, Professor Méndez? By that time he couldn't make anything out with his eyes, but his inner vision was faster than the speed of light. He talked to me about his friendship with Alfonso Reyes and about how he memorized page after page by the writer from Monterrey. In the afternoon, which was morning in his cosmos, he would repeat them like Hamlet reciting his endless speeches. Seeing Borges was like meeting Funes the Memorious in the flesh. The bell rings. We depart, saying to each other "See you on Monday," "Have a good weekend," and the like.

Well, here I am seated on this animal with rubber feet and round reins. Now, I'll ride him on home on the laminated trail. It'll take me a half hour to get there. Ah, God in Heaven, I need to lay this skeleton to rest, with its aches in every joint, along with its fluids and its skin and who knows what else. Despite the fact that I'm riding along in the traffic with this contraption, another recollection from my days as a scamp back there in El Claro is fluttering around in my head. While Jeremiah talked to himself, this jumbled matter spilled forth from my inner whirlpool with its backward movement drowning me in hidden subconscious realms. It whirls me around, it pounds me, it envelops me frantically in a world of dreams, others and my own. It's probably true that this is all the result of tremendous exhaustion, which is where the wild fever to tell stories unchecked comes from, leaving my blood like chocolate ready to boil over.

The fact is that the trees that lined the ditch next to my house made of ocotillos, with an artificial lagoon in the shade where both neighbors and strangers came to water their horses, served as a stage for all kinds of things: friendly meetings, arguments, love trysts, playing field, and so on. We would be right there as astute voyeurs to see young teachers from the Cultural Mission bathe themselves. Women and men would cavort together in mixed company, their genitals covered only by a strip of cloth and their butts in full view. It was a joy to see how they would fondle each other, running races and bumping into each other on purpose. I lay in wait in the bushes, over to the side where the young women who taught us little kids the alphabet had left their clothes. The prettiest and most charming of the lot arrived, the one who was really the nicest. Without seeing me, she took off what little clothes she was wearing. Then for the first time in my life my virgin eyes had revealed to them a pair of tits and a cunt that even Marilú Monreal with all her fame would have liked to have for one Sunday. That whole night of my anxious youth, I thrashed my arms and legs about and writhed in an intense dream filled with insomnia and that gorgeous little girl who taught the alphabet. Her heavenly tits and cunt had taken possession of my retinas.

The ditch I mentioned had water in it for about three weeks of the year. Then the water masters would divert its course toward another distant channel so other lands would be irrigated. Thus we would have weeks of continuous bathing, but also prolonged exposure to blowing dust and heat without the benefit of the desired liquid. We were toads for a few days and then we would be skunks for the rest of the time.

Hunting tigers, lions, or any other kind of beast must be exciting. But in terms of risk and maximum excitement, the intense and thrilling itch of getting the best of a rattlesnake is not to be beat, at least unless they strike first with their four half-moon syringes. Professionals know how to hunt them with a minimum of serious risk. We went about it completely lacking in any sense. Mario, my cousin, would grab the gila monsters, minidragons, by the very tip of their tail. Since they are clumsy, they would bend themselves upward. Just as they were about to bite his hand, Mario would knock them on the head with a heavy stick. The bite of these animals is a free ticket to the cemetery. For some unknown and mysterious reason, there is an irresistible temptation to stone toads. We would steal chicken eggs in broad daylight from right under the noses of housewives, just for the pure pleasure of seeing them get mad enough to shit their pants.

I'm almost home now. The traffic fills the streets with gasoline vapors. Over the years I've been able to subordinate the anger of my Sonoran humanity to a certain gentle demeanor, despite the savagery that lies at the core of city life. Nevertheless, amidst the squeal of tire, goose bumps, my hair standing on end, insult-honking horns, the wail of wounded ambulances, and other disasters proper to the urban nightmare, I yield to thinking as a form of open escape. In order to accomplish this, I stand aside for what is fighting to rise to the surface from bygone days. I shout like Tarzan if I feel like it, just so I won't feel left out among so many brainless madmen rushing around like greyhounds. I finally make it home.

Take it easy, don't get up, forget about your books and scribbling. I'll get you some pills. You should see how you look, like you really need to see a doctor. A doctor? Doctors just help you die. We'll just see, that is, if we don't go blind. It was a mistake to promise to deliver that essay about the revolution of language. Like that famous Don Lolito, I go crazy on my own. Then there's the book waiting for me that I want to submit to a competition. Why bother to send another one. You're right, because the first two weren't even among the finalists. I was raised in Mexico, but I can't hope to win a literary prize there for two reasons: one because I was born in the United States, and two because what I write isn't worth a hill of beans. Here in Gringolandia they think I'm crazy because I write in Spanish, and so long prizes, fellowships, the lot. Forget them, you'll see how I plop down in the middle of them one fine day. You've got no complaint because you've gone farther than you ever thought you would, so what more do you want. Well, for starters I'd like to feel better. If I can't write this weekend, what will I do about that project to write something on Don Camilo vs. Arizona. I want to have a good nap, but not to close my eyes so I can see a parade of faces and things I don't understand. And you talk endlessly in your sleep. You say such strange things in your ravings, that is when you're not spewing forth one vulgarity after the other of the worst kind. You're such a barbarian. The kids can tell you don't want to see a doctor. That's why they don't take care of themselves. Come on now, go to sleep, your fever's real high. Look how it's morning and they've got handcuffs on Chuvili and Toñón and they're whipping them on their backs with the reins. Sweet Jesus, now you're going to start babbling. Never mind Chuvili and Toñón, just get some rest so you'll feel better. They're both to blame: Chuvili because he held on to the leg and Toñón because he's the one that killed the cow.

It's the same cops leading the prisoners. No, that's not right, because Trots is not one of them. He fell off his horse and was crushed to death riding drunk in a terrain full of holes. Ah, look, there's Lenchón, he's got the Devil's own mouth on him. The march is on foot. They shove the rustlers along, but they can hardly walk because they are shackled like oxen. Get going, you sons of bitches, move it, come on. We follow along beside them, a horde of kids and a couple of adults. From time to time, the cops lash out at us, cracking their whips in the air, but we fall back in on top of them like a pack of yapping dogs. But what the hell, doesn't anyone show these creeps how to behave. What's so funny about it is that the ones everybody's calling hustlers are Toñón and Chuvili. Toñón has a long gray beard, and he's a big broad-shouldered titan who's as gentle as a lamb. He never raises his voice and barely grimaces sadly. By contrast, Chuvili is a thorny branch. He's short of stature and so thin his meatless ribs show. Malnutrition and rotgut known in those parts as shit have aged him. Every so often they beat him in the streets and he comes back for more. He talks like a two-year old and he always has trouble with a couple of letters like *R, S, D,* and so on. If we've got some distance between us and him we shout, "Chinaman, Chinaman, show us your pigtails, Chinaman." Then he gets as mad as a wet hen. Tarungas, Chilo, and Lenchón are a symphony of swear words and gestures. Chuvili throws himself to the ground in front of them and refuses to get up "even if you sons of bitches slit my throat." He's dangling loosely from Toñón's left arm. Lenchón measures out an arm's length of the reins, doubles it three times, and strikes the ground with force to test it and then shouts at Chuvili who's coughing and swallowing dust. Get up you fucking bag of bones or I'll make you get up, damn bag of TB. Neither you nor your bitch of a mother can make me get up, you fucking creep, you're nothing but a tongue. Tarungas Ruiz laughs quietly like he always does. Chilo, the other cop, is laughing so hard he's spitting all over the place. Lenchón is wild with anger and he strikes Chuvili three times with the whip and leaves him writhing like a snake. Stop it, Lenchón you bastard, you're nothing but a big shit, taking advantage of me like this, you fucking pig. Just so you'll know, I'm your father and I fuck your mother. The lawman this time raises the lasso even higher so it looks like the claw of a tyrannosaurus about to tear Chuvili to shreds. But Captain Ruiz, alias Tarungas, yells at him. Don't do it, shitface. Use your head, you animal. You've got to respect him for what he is, do you hear me. If you kill him, we'll all end up in jail and there's no point in that. Well, you know what, Don Tarungas, there's your fucking prisoner, so go shove him up your ass. Ruiz puts his right hand on his gun without drawing it and shoves Lenchón roughly with his left one. Take back what you just said, Lenchón, or you're going to end up with an extra eye. Lenchón backs down. What do you mean take back what I said and who's taking pictures. Say you're sorry, you creep. OK, you're the boss, so tell me how to use my head so this spoiled brat'll walk without beating his brains out, which is what he deserves. The one who's spoiled is your fuck of a mother, you shit. Shut up, Chuvili, there's a reason why you're under arrest. Tarungas Ruiz whispers some instructions in Lenchón's ear. Lenchón smiles from ear to ear and his eyes become beady with delight. There's a silent pause. The atmosphere trembles with expectation under the solar reverberation and nothing moves. Chuvili's lying on the ground. Toñón, half bent over, shows his broad shoulders. Suddenly in the flash of a second, Lenchón gathers all his strength together and lands the lasso with all his might on Toñón's kidneys. The giant races off violently with Chuvili on his back. The lawman manages to land another blow of the lasso on the back of the terrified giant. The deep groan that the pain brings forth seems to work like a jet to propel him backwards. He's stood Chuvili on his feet like a puppet and made him stride along. The two are running side by side. The bystanders and the policemen double over laughing. Us kids spend the rest of the day laughing reconstructing each scene and imitating Chuvili: "You dirty motherfucking sons of bitches."

My God, what a hateful fever. Instead of getting better it gets worse. I can't wait for dawn to come, so I can see you conscious without such a high fever. If you'd just stop mumbling so many weird things. You keep right on talking, and you toss around and fling your arms in the air. Tomorrow I'm going to take you to the doctor for sure. Here, take some more aspirins.

"**Literature** is life molded in letters, sublime or otherwise. The same is true of reason, which embodies itself in noble, poetic concepts, which extend themselves as far as understanding is capable of grasping, which engages in an exploratory rumination for purposes of confronting the crudity of a body of animate clay, one dripping in blood, made into a pool of sweat, smelling of shit, with putrid feet, tortured by being punched in the nose and kicked in the butt and genitals, torn between convulsions, gasps and moans of pleasure, contrite and sanctified—or rather, so much the worse, find him filled with ironic contentment, now an overbearing political figure incarnate, because despite his being an abominable assassin, he passes as a hero before a mankind drunk with imbecility and on a high resulting from vain self-interest—the same thinking animal multiplied dizzyingly on the face of the earth, speaks out, moves vertically, and repeats, repeats until he has deluded himself and has deceived fools with the ears of puppets, supposedly in concert with God and has been given the power to pass judgment on reasons of the spirit and human attitudes. And should it be to his pleasure, he has the power to be the divine arm that strikes out with bombardments, shellings, planned famine against anyone who denies or works against the authority that he has come to enjoy by the grace and consent of the Almighty. This too is literature, an entity that can't stand the breath with which he envelops the purest and most beautiful words that will come to make up the lines of the prettiest and most ingenious of poems. Beyond refracting the attitudes and realities he stumbles upon, it falls within the scope of the literary intent of this highly evolved being who imitates the gait of a monkey to demonstrate as well the inner universe signified by imagination, capable of recreating fantasy in multiple and infinite forms.

"So then, who can deprive me of the will to nourish myself with torrents of letters and to make a place for myself, if I so chose and will it out of absurd, audacious, unheard of, legitimate, or bastard pretense, in the great realm of letters, sheltered by the Spanish language descended from by now a centuries-old cultivation along the border and out of the world of the Mexican desert that lies contiguous with that of Arizona?

"It should be known that among vast ranges of dunes, a rider in this devil's own wandering, with a saguaro as a spear and this daring with which I protect my mettle from viperlike attacks as a shield. I demand from those of you who do indeed deny us with your indifference and mean skepticism to desist in impeding the dedication that drives me with its cries to cross literary arms in this tournament in which Spanish and Latin American knights take the measure of their valor and their prowess. Were it not thus so, I conjure you by the honor of Cervantes himself to come forth to joust with me on whatever terms may please your industry. I turn this my trusty steed over to the battle, in so far as I am on this battlefield for at least two weighty reasons. Who, then, shall cast me forth from these dominions? These dominions that are mine, by God, by inheritance and not by theft!"

Now look here, you've been having these damned fevers going on a week and you insist on continuing to spend eight lousy hours a day working yourself to death, work more appropriate for mules burros elephants and oxen like a bunch of real studs even though it's Saturday and you could rest a bit but now here you go saying you want to go to the fair hell! we're really done with it no man I'm not doing that bad I just made a long pee and now I'm hungry enough to eat a horse and I'm strong enough to go anywhere I can get myself a couple of meat burros with chile or roast beef ones and for dessert some corn tamales and some real refried beans with green chile sauce so who hit you sweetheart you've got to give the patient what he wants and the simple fact is that at the fair aside from rides and people who are the theater and the circus in action there are all those food stands that set my teeth going like crazy my innards just love those Chicano fiestas I guess there's nothing really wrong with me because if you eat and pee you're fine as a flea we're both made out of the same stuff because I tell you over and over to look out for your health and security just like Fidelito and I are brothers in Christ and you the same as me and you let my words of advice go in one ear and out the other after all we've got today off come on let's just run by and we'll be right back after all a fever is a good friend it burns the bad humors off and if now and then an ugly Christian gets carried off it doesn't have anything to do with me that's what they say you've got to learn to love God in this green land of the Gringo yum yum yummmmm what great down-home cooking with food like this even a fever's great before we leave we'll take a look at everything let's see what catches your attention in particular among all this mass of common people jumbled together in crowds well I happen to note that since this is a neighborhood a part of town with a lot of down-and-out people as far as economics go well it's like they correspond to what is called the mere masses it sounds kind of fucked up and look at them you can see their dried-up faces their eyes at half-mast walking like they were shackled just like the loads they put on their backs and how do they get to laugh in English the whole business goes to hell the poor kids neither laugh nor scream sure you're right the other day we were in an expensive and elegant supermarket bursting at the seams with nice well-dressed people somewhere else right where the bigwigs live those who call the tune smiling men and women with their own or false teeth very young or real old the whole ball of wax or whatever what do you expect let's see what you deal with in that globe sitting on top of your neck the idea that if you're poor you're as ugly as borrowing money no hold on don't say that those are fucked-up things way over to the fucking distance only to fuck a great fucking number of people only because they are not fucking good don't fuck me with fucking little things that are rumors of sons of bitches reason fast and fucking well shut up you're fucking the language of daddy Cortés the real poor are ugly because they don't use makeup they get all covered with warts they smell bad they don't dress right and they don't even wear clothes the right size they experience hunger they lose their color they wear dirty rags they have perennial colds they spit up colored phlegm when they smile they look angry they turn on each other they half die from the cold from the heat from attacks of sadness they go into rages of anger envy hatred frustration one of their eyes waters they get white spots on the skin they get fucked here down there the rich screw them they go to the Galapagos islands without a mask since they are iguanas dragons lizards if everything were turned upside down inside out the overbearing hotshots would scare their dad Beelzebub the pack of stuck-ups would look like they were dead with their bristly snout their vacant eyes their scrofulous scaly skin their shitty asshole oozing miasmas in abundance ladies going around without boob supporters new clothes makeup hairdos relaxation they would be like lost frogs terrifying monstrous by contrast the women dying from hunger plastered with makeup wigs high heels well-fed store-bought teeth good-smelling their tits silicon-inflated liposuctioned their double chins pruned away their skin stretched tight as a drum forest dusk in color their legs armpits pubic areas shaved you bet their picture appears on magazine covers with their butts hanging out to the four winds just a tuft of coverage you know where suspended from a string half-eaten by the holy assorum that not even a leash for a pig with a petal on each nipple coquettish modest it's a cinch they'll win beauty contests a bigmouthed man with a television for brains and a frog in his throat that croaks and croaks sounding just like copulation the big-ass image rock-and-roll industry come on you sweet young things of high-born artistic lineage little rich girls crème de la crème here on the screen yes yes their smooth fat buttocks millions and fame there they come hand in hand with the same old eternal line not even they themselves believe it oh sure they spew out their crap and then congratulate each other among them the invisible man covers himself with lime dust out of shame out of ridicule they stone him if he says anything what laughter if he writes anything they clean themselves with ink go to Gringoland you Indians brownies whiteys ignorant bleary-eyed the cake is only for our family alone it's just that ah so you wanna fight huh? OK Napo Nerón lieutenant general Judas go get 'em sick 'em woof woof woof starving wetbacks chase them back to their stinking towns come on you border agents with your cute new rifles with telescopic lenses with smart bullets sure it's an electronic game deer decked out in sandals baskets wearing hats bang bang bang yacka yacka yacka you're fucked little deer raging river swallow them up that's the way bravo bravo we don't want them around here hunger is what drives them from over there real dregs they've got oil so why mess with them what jobs? our money to the U.S. to Switzerland for you here is nothing so take as much to support yourselves here we come over to earn dollars and to improve your race hordes from the south invade us give to Caesar what belongs to Caesar sons of Marilyn Monroe this is Aztlán just give it time you'll see ah so democracy? they'll get to vote when grandmothers give birth and let's get the queers in on it more votes OK brother OK let's go tie that tongue it would've been better if you hadn't eaten for a week I'll read the Bible to you so you'll calm down you get going on one of your outbursts and not even Job himself could put up with you.

You sure look sick, what's the matter, it looks like you've been working too hard, your classes and your students during the day and then you're busy with your writing at night, so much activity has left you baggy-eyed and distracted as usual. The kids stare at you. Our daughter came to me real worried and asked me if you'd gone crazy. They hear you talking to yourself. Yes, I am a bit feverish. There's nothing new in my talking to myself. When I'm writing I like to try the sounds out and to check out the many meanings that arise when words are combined with each other. I have the impression that lately things from my inner cosmos were getting all mixed up together along with things from the real world, and I end up confused with so much of a mishmash.

I'm writing now about the year '53, yes, 1953, and it's just as if I were reliving it. Despite the fact it was such a tough, difficult year, it grabs me with great intensity. My ex-fellow workers have appeared in sharp outlines. It is enough to tell how each day I feel my body fractured and exhausted by extremely hard construction work for eight hours a day. There are about a hundred of us. Did I say are or were? It's the same thing. See, certain earthly concepts, necessarily localist, come to have a time imposed on them where the past and the future flow together in a present that is inalterable because it is perennial, one that is alien to planetary rotations and systems. You should take a couple of aspirins to calm yourself down a bit. Every time you start up with your strange ideas I get worried. Bah, you're just like Fidel, who thinks my interest in writing is nothing but sheer madness. The real kicker is that I am also involved in trying to write an essay on the power of the misfortune in giving life and death to languages, even though it's not turning out how I want it to. I'm a mess intellectually and artistically, in this literature game I've entered into without permission, by hook or by crook and maybe like a jerk. Fidel, you were saying? Yes, Fidel. The other day I forgot I had run into him in the fictitious year of 1953, which is where I situate the events of a matter that I am expounding on, or messing up if you want, right now too, and before I knew it I was talking details over with him about the visit here in Tucson of Camilo José Cela, when he was my guest, our guest, in February 1987. What Fidel are you talking about? Don't tell me Castro from Cuba. No, no, this Fidel was a mason, someone who worked with me. We worked in various cities. We used to use an old Ford to save money, taking turns with each trip to a distant site. We would rent a dump together. Since Fidel was a Holy Roller, he never drank or got into trouble, which allowed me to write in peace. He was a good friend and had a sense of humor. Why do you say was, because he's dead maybe. Yes, I think he died a while back, in 1990, barely two years ago. The fact is I predicted his death in this immersion of mine in the past, in a curious conversation in which he questioned my intuitive power. I can't follow you. Are you talking about a literary character or a flesh and blood person. The two in one. It turns out that last week, and this in the plane of reality, ahem, I ran into Fidel's brother-in-law when I went to the store to buy bread and milk. He's in his sixties like me and I barely recognized him after thirty years. I asked him so many questions about Fidel, after so many years of not seeing him, that he had no choice but to let it all out and told me all sorts of things about the great old guy. Who would've believed it, he left his family when he was an old man, his wife and children and even his roots. To be more precise, he left his crotchety old woman for a budding nymphet and they went to Hawaii to enjoy their lovemaking and to do what they wanted to, taking advantage of the pressing demand for masons. Samuel, the brother-in-law, explained it to me in these terms. Fidelito was such a fanatic in his religion that once when his son came home in a euphoric mood and carrying a colored TV set, Fidel told him that it was a sin and without even taking the cellophane wrapper off they tossed it into the garbage. Fidel died over there, buried in strange ground. It seems that the girl dropped him for a young man her age. Listen, writer, mason, professor, family man and I don't know how many other things, maybe your students keep you too busy and, combined with all the things you plan on doing, your rest and your health leave you and so you end up going around like a madman. I'm not going around like a madman, I am a madman, but very consciously nevertheless; and my situation doesn't harm a soul, even if you and my children are affected a little bit by it or a lot by my passion from drawing stories from the loom of life. In the classes I teach I derive pleasure from each and every novel and author we study. This is sure a unique world. Structure, style, theme, and plot as well as various other features are worth seeing so you can have a ball learning things. Besides successive literary periods and schools, there's something like an indelible torrent in which history leaves its mark on us in a completely natural manner while at the same time it predisposes us to perceive more clearly the way in which it unfolds. I have doctoral and M.A. students and others in my classes. On more than one occasion my students have asked me where I got my doctorate. I tell them laughing that it's from the University of Santa María de las Piedras. When I tell them the truth, that I only have six years of grade school in a small communal village in Sonora called El Claro, they can't believe it and think I'm kidding them. They know that in the hierarchy of university professors I'm at the top as a full-time professor. So that between this upward extreme and the other end, which has its roots in my reality as a self-taught peasant, there is a whole, extensive trajectory, filled with contradictory anecdotes and circumstances that nourish my anemic gifts as a writer. During the two weeks that Don Camilo and I talked day and night, Don Camilo never put his notebook down, his pen always poised and he asking question after question about the Sonoran Desert, local speech, and so many other things. He wrote everything right down, saying over and over again: How lovely, how lovely. Trying not to fall into the sin of being presumptuous and with a modest manner, since in a sense I was giving him lessons about these topics, I once said to him: Don Camilo, I'm nothing more than a Sonoran peasant. And he answered me by saying: Man, I'm nothing more than a Galician peasant. Well, what did you talk to Fidel about back there, as you said, in 1953, with respect to anecdotes Don Camilo told you in February 1987 when he visited us. Blessed be God, we'll just have to see how this book turns out and then we'll see what other themes you find to drown your little brain in mercilessly. Well, so I remembered about the time I talked to Miguelito, Isabelita, and the others about their adventures when they were kids. According to Camilo José Cela, when he was a child he and his gang set up a fart bank. This involved stuffing themselves with a lot of hot food that produces gases, and they helped it along by drinking quantities of cold water. They would have already set aside fat-bellied bottles with tops that could be fastened on easily and that closed tight. When it was time they fought over who would go first. With their pants down around their ankles and accompanied by explosions appropriate to balky heavy-laden burros, each one would make his fartsome deposit, filling bottle after bottle. The feline agility with which they opened and closed such unique savings accounts was something to see. Then they would place their windy treasures of supersmelling essences on strategic corners and they would roll on the ground laughing at the thought of the faces of the grandmothers, mothers, aunts, and servants when they went to put up the preserves they had prepared for the winter months. Boy, the stories Don Camilo would tell. That old guy is a swell human being and he can afford the luxury of making fun of himself and being serious as the mood suits him because he's the type who always comes off fine. Everything would be fine, writing is your vocation after all, but what's bad about it is I can see you're so preoccupied, so filled with sadness, just now when life is smiling on you. Well, I don't know. I think in the case of those of us who take up writing our subconscious, which functions as a storage room for traumas, doesn't work. In every story we tell we stumble upon some hidden wound and it erupts. Sometimes those wounds show up masked as literature, as characters the author has neither invited nor considered and it really intrigues me, why they come, who put them there, why they invade someone else's writing. Ah, no, that's not possible, they're all your pipe dreams and none of this is by accident. It's got to be the result of exhaustion, fever, or something . . . and what does this story mean anyway. The point is that among all these people I'm involved with in the construction of several very large buildings, in the midst of a tremendous uproar, shouts, screeching, the noise of hammers, motors, machines, elevators, and what not going on, I ran into a sixty-year-old man, exactly my age now, so he looked at me out of the corner of his eye with malice, openly mocking me. Now he ups and tells me that he came barging into my story because a dead man's rantings and ravings plopped him down there, with his mind running all over the place in its flight from his fevered burning heat. So there he is, Cruz Ramos in his present form, an old man in our midst, but we've all regressed to our youth. I didn't go up to this old geezer from Sinaloa, because if he was as funny as hell when he was a young man, he's intolerable now. Sure, he's a nice person, no doubt about it, and perhaps even funny, but he wormed his way into my exclusive cosmos without me even foreseeing it and that upsets me, driving me crazy. No one does that to me. I got the idea to kill him, real quick, rub him out, and that would be the end of that, but the old joker with his eyes covered with cataracts started to cry and explained to me: In the same way I came from nowhere, riding out this fever that will carry me to my grave any minute now; I can see all of you again nevertheless, unforgettable friends, a real blessing for my memory. Little brother, death is about to carry me off. But, listen, you writer of nonsense, do you remember that little brunette you took to the dance once? Yes, Professor, Grace, real cute, and in case you don't remember, you unarmed her jealous boyfriend when he went after you with the knife. You're crazy, Cruz Ramos, that business about her boyfriend threatening me is a lie, or why would I have taken her to the Flamingo, if my memory serves me right. Yes, try to remember, I'm talking about Chucho Grijalva, who followed you into the bathroom with a knife in his hand, and you turned around and looked him in the face real happy like and said to him, You're Grijalva, from the same place I'm from, right? Your father and mine are friends, from the same town, even though each one went his own way years ago. My dad told me to check in with you, so you know, you can count on me as a friend. When you left, Chucho gave a short laugh and said, "My sainted father saved that dude, you know the old guy kicked off a couple of months ago." Yeah, sure, I found out that same night that Chucho was Graciela's boyfriend. She took her time about telling me. Later, real timidlike, Grijalva put his gutslicer away shaking his head, and there you were lickety-split, well into it, dancing "Jesusita en Chihuahua" cheek to cheek with Gracielita, damn. The ink in my pen doesn't know anything about what you're telling me, and the same goes for your being here, you damn gate-crasher. His belly was shaking from laughter and ole Cruz Ramos's face looked as sly as it could, which left me empty-handed trying to figure out how I had lost my grip on this stray literature that fails to match any genre. Brooks and bicks, if you want to know. And of course, there the critics are, ready to jump in and tear apart anything that looks like a book, and then in a flash, all the way to the ground we go! The worst of the lot are novelists turned reviewers, because they chastise their own limitations mercilessly when they find them in the work of others. Thy will be done, My Lord, on my compadre's burros. I don't like what you're telling me one bit. Please, Miguel, stop writing for once and stay home from the university tomorrow. Try to get rid of the fever, because it's running very high. If my defenses can't free me from something so insignificant wherever I am, then they can just get the hell out of here, because I'm not going to abandon what I've got to do. No matter how exhausted I am, I'm going to finish this business. I have so many commitments to finish jokes like this one that I sometimes long to return to renting my body out from the neck down and leave this poor head of mine without violent jolts and the boiling over of heated brains. I can be in many places and epochs at the same time and now that so many exploitable levels have come together for me I'm not about to be the one caught in a corner. I'm an expert at doing in labyrinths, along with their Cretan bulls. Take these aspirins and this tea, which is good and hot. Calm down and stop talking and thinking and get some rest. It's midnight and I'm going to rub your forehead. That's it, go to sleep now.

What's wrong with that boy? His shirt's getting all bloodstained. Look, his right shoulder's bleeding. It sure is. It's that bucket full of mixed cement that he rests on his shoulder to carry it to the masons that has made a mess of it, no doubt about it. Cement mixed with lime and sand is very heavy, and he's been at the same thing for ten days. He's a real hard worker. No, he's not the only one. The other laborers have the same problems. Well, yes, but the others have a lot of experience, and besides they're older and tougher. This one's a young kid just in from the country, from some communal farm. Brother, the truth of the matter is that it isn't good for us to have him here, because if he bangs himself or gets sick and someone reports us, where will that leave us, Brother Beto. I don't know, Brother Chema. All I know is that the kid needs a hand. He's very proud, and without a job he'll starve to death. He's not one of those to stick his hat out and roll his eyes so you'll give him alms. Well, then, he can go back to his family in Mexico, Brother Alberto, and raise goats and pigs. Our job is to contract workers for construction sites, and we aren't some kind of charitable institution, so get that in your head. Brother in Christ, hallelujah!, but he does as much or more work than the others, and he sends his family whatever he's got left over from his check, praise the Lord!, rather than shelling it out for booze like the others. Church and business don't always go well together, brother, but if it's a matter of something Christian for the health of the soul, we've got to find something else for him to do. Just look at him, brother, can't you see how every time he comes back he fills that thing up with mixture and then hoists it up on his shoulder, it starts to bleed as though his veins were bursting.

The two Hallelujah brothers, both in their thirties and worker contractors for construction sites, ordered the boy not to climb the ladder anymore with the sheet metal container filled with cement mixture slung over his shoulder, dripping sweat and blood.

Without his shirt on you could see the wound, a small volcano overflowing with yellowish-tinted red lava. It was obviously swollen. Even though the kid refused to see a doctor before his eight-hour shift was up, Mr. Beto made him go with him. Brother Chema, his back toward the stubborn boy, signaled to his partner to understand by shaking his head that he was losing his time on "monkey business," to which Brother Alberto answered, his seal face glowing: Brother, this kid's got balls.

He took him to a small clinic. The white interior exuded the brightness and the smells common to hygienic places. After waiting a few minutes they were seen by a young doctor, tall and jovial, who set about examining the novice worker. Brother Alberto served as interpreter. A very young and pretty blonde nurse came in carrying a tray of instruments and medicines, and she nodded and smiled as she spoke with a serene expression. She saw the wound and shivered slightly. Her eyes met those of the young man, and she smiled at him with an innocent tenderness full of friendliness. Scream and cry if you want, the doctor told him, but don't jerk your body so it won't hurt more than it has to. This whole area is infected. You're allergic to penicillin, but since you're young and strong, thanks to these medicines and assistance from your constitution you'll be better than new. The blond doctor put his big hands into action. He squeezed harder and harder, and pus and blood flowed out of the small crater until the color of putrefaction disappeared and the wound showed only the red liquid of life. They proceeded to wash the wound, wrap it in gauze, and bind it with a bandage. Intense pain showed on the face of the young man. His eyes were dry, and he'd swallowed quite a few tears. The doctor was passingly intrigued. The boy neither moved nor uttered a word. Mr. Beto smiled, "This kid's really something." Tiny tears formed in the blue pupils of the nurse who was, after all, new at her job.

The medicine, the attention, the reaction of his body, and a couple of days were enough to patch up his shoulder, which despite all was strong. He had emerged victorious from what seemed symbolically to be the tribute life exacted from him in exchange for his entrance into the workers' union a little shy of being fifteen years old.

The rough construction work was for the time being his only alternative, knowing full well about those who collapse with cramps because of sunstroke, either to die or be blinded by the sun, not to mention many other risks, along with foolish antics on payday in the heat of drinking and fooling around.

Two weeks previously he had appeared before a superintendent of local education to request the necessary permit to engage in easy indoor labor despite still being of school age. The big shot told him in academic Spanish, in something more than an ironic tone, No, we're not in Mexico here, where laws don't count. We are in the United States, where the law is the law and must be strictly obeyed. This is the land of democracy and liberty.

From that early day in his life he swore to himself that he was "the kid with a will" who would attain goals as high and as honorable as the best of his fellow generation. He already knew about hunger, blood, pus, and he would know whatever he would have to.

So, when he left that Mr. Superintendent's office, he left floating in the air some apparently mysterious words: I don't care who cares, but I'll forge my own future by the sweat of my brow. My God, you really have a fever and you're thrashing about and saying one delirious thing after another!

I'm a mason and a poet-writer with the agility of my hands and the disciplined rigor of my mind with a mixture that gets as hard as stone plus eternal chains of bricks I have built homes and universities at the same time I have put forth galaxies of words chains of words in a procession of syllables following penetrating and labyrinthine thoughts I forge exemplary constructions to the sound of poems in verses while simultaneously walls and buildings arise stories novels poems and an endless number of projects eight hours of hard labor leave me silent my hands my back my whole being aches nevertheless invention persists and persists a new wall looks solid and airy the letters glow in an illusory mosaic now I sleep inertly worn-out in absolute repose deep in my subconscious chimeric visions sing me lullabies I see myself as a writer alongside famous authors they address me I pretend to run away flee a setting that is alien to me but they really do treat me with deference young journalists girls boys smilingly interview me without scorn is it possible I am the perfect impostor I proclaim that I am this and that and there are those who believe me but I was only playing ah they take my picture I smile cynically Maestro! your literary work . . . who called me Maestro which work gentlemen one of the two winners of the national prize for literature . . . is . . . who is that old man who walks like a laborer with rough hands who is receiving that medal he's bursting with happiness he is a lonely child who finally finds some friends like himself even if for only a moment as shining and fleeting as a bolt of lightning tomorrow will be another day I will once again build with my hands and I will create with my mind from the scaffolding I still see a humanity that passes by indifferent to the cosmos ideals decked out with elegance they appear to be solvent and well fed they usually look at me with a touch of pity and I in turn express for them with a smile a certain commiseration some walk with the pride of someone with education of means and strong while I proclaim exclusively a sea of letters poor laborer they probably say he has neither capital nor property they haven't the faintest idea how happy a dreamer usually feels who constructs fantasy motifs from reality to make fun of his suffering and who cries over the happiness for those who so blithely and with so much power dig the grave of illusion when they no longer desire a single thing whose price is not found on a sticker hey chump it's time to eat what the hell you don't have a fuck of an idea get off your high horse go screw your mother you bastard son of a rotten bitch how quick you learn you jerk yes sir and no one gives you the time of day because they'll kick you in the snout well yes kiss my ass on the green grass if they don't like it they can eat it what the fuck the guys don't screw you over because they think you're a real card funny as hell you sure can dish it out in Pachuco lingo hey you got it quick as a wink anyway yellow fellow don't try to give them a rough time or they'll get you good if their balls decide so what do you mean balls ass more like it I'll fight with one arm tied behind my back and to any dude stomped by the devil I'll give him a chance to give me a kick on the balls you know the balls you crush but then they're as fresh as ever you who call yourself a poet and in the air you fixed them jerk me off by hand without any of those damn plots early in the morning with the balls fried I'm nothing of the sort and I won't ever be what I carry in my pants is for the good of you know who my little dove in your aunt's shack you can get a swell fuck OK that's it for now what the heck old buddy that's how a bunch of those masons talk well after all of that who stinks more miners or masons who knows I think they're all about the same.

OK, now I've really had enough of this. Tomorrow you're going to the doctor even if I have to handcuff you. Come on, swallow some more pills and go to sleep.

"**Without** literature, a language is hollow. An empty language is like a human being with a sick heart, like a tree with fragile roots that do not go down deep. A people whose language leaves no trace in literature will be incapable of preserving its memory. In the end, cultural amnesia will erase from its character the marks that only a spirit that is well nourished in history and sublime events can conjure up, from the time of its ancestors up to the very vanguard of its days. The loss of respect and dignity at the hands of those who belong to a different culture, who are proud because they are overbearing, hidden behind shields of justice and religiosity, so that ignominy, the spiritual cancer of humanity, may perpetuate itself in the enslavement of the defenseless, cannot take place if there is a living culture, one that is deeply rooted and with a clear history before it.

"It is usually the case that the literary phenomenon functions like an entity that searches out all over the place some brain on which to latch itself and then from within submit it to its authority in order to command it with imperious cruelty to give life and death to it so that it can manifest itself in texts and not die, by the virtue and grace of those eyes that like dikes give way to the widening of its currents. When I become exhausted down to the very last letter in this undertaking, I fill with rage and come to think that literature chooses us who are ingenuous and the most foolish of the lot, knowing that we can be persuaded because we are weak. That is why we heed its charges, writing from one turmoil to the next, because from one clarification to the next we exchange hours of gall for a bittersweet piece of bread. This business of writing is quite funny, not to say ironic, even when we are not men of letters in the strictest sense of the term. What else is literature for humanity but its shadow, since only we living beings project it. Those people without a "shadow" live as though dead. It is preferable to die in a rage and out of exhaustion than to consent to the historical death for our children and their descendants. After all, what is illegible because it is trivial is better off feeding rats and cockroaches. . . ."

Brother, it's already five in the morning and you're awake. We've got to arm ourselves with a good breakfast and get something ready to eat for lunch. Time to rush off to erect walls with heavy materials and to do the work of cranes for eight hours at a stretch. Quit screwing man and stay in bed. You're really going to kill yourself if you go up on the scaffolding half out of your mind. The truth is I don't know if what you're writing is worth the trouble, if it's a pack of your buffoonish and childish nonsense, after all, spending night after night painting spider legs, what for, let's see. I don't know either, brother, I really don't. Let's see, why didn't you sleep three hours at least. Because I rode a very spirited black horse named Chronos. I dug the spurs in until his flanks bled and his mouth frothed, and in only a matter of minutes we were flying over the hours of this night. I really don't understand all this gibberish of yours. You ought to go get born all over again so you can receive the true baptism in my church, because something tells me you'd make a fine preacher. I'll begin with the choir girls. Pipe down. You're full of Satan now. You speak with wisdom at night, like a God-fearing man, and during the day you become foul-mouthed like a devil. You'd better get married so you won't sin in thought. Choir girls, spare me. Fidel, at night I talk with books, and I try to seduce the muses so they will bless me or whatever pleases them. They're women, after all, and are after something. . . . I deal with laborers during the day: masons, carpenters, peons who, in short, have their own speech and customs. Without even thinking about it I act like them when I'm with them because I don't consider myself different. I was born a miner, I was raised a peasant in Mexico, and here alongside wetbacks I have done hard labor in the fields, picking lettuce, cotton, wielding the short hoe. I've been a construction worker in so many different places, and moreover ever since I was born I've been and will be until my death and beyond a writer by the grace of the Almighty and the midnight oil I've burned. And don't you doubt for a moment that I'll end up a distinguished university professor. At least you're not a violent madman, and as far as I'm concerned you can be Neptune if you want. But it sure seems weird to me that whenever we reach a work site and you mingle with that bunch of devils, you're the swearingest Pachuco around. Well, why shouldn't I talk dirty. It doesn't faze that pack of louts. They respect you because they know you're a Holy Roller. Children, women, and men of the cloth rarely get bothered because they are by nature peaceful and inoffensive, even if they are dumb, dumb most of the time. Now, brother in Christ, let's have a super-size cup of coffee, half a dozen scrambled eggs with sausage and refried beans, along with some tortillas. That'll keep me from going to sleep and falling off the scaffolds. I could probably even walk on air as well as on water.

You're a simpleton, no doubt about it. I'll drive now, or you'll continue to be confused by what you write and you'll fall off the black burro you rode last night. You like roasted goat, brother. It's getting late for you because you haven't heard me talk broncolike. People are still sound asleep at this hour. Those who are in the street are half-asleep, just look at them, we're the only ones who have to bust our guts in killer construction work, what the fuck. Well, here we are at the site. Now we're going to ride demons that look like black goats, brother, to take us across hell itself during these hours. There's no other way to describe this sun beating down on us. Even your words seem to get blisters just like nothing. The only thing that'll keep you from dying from impatience or from the heat are the red-hot jokes and dirty stories that even the carpenters laugh about, not to mention the rivers of sweat that keep us from roasting to death. Hold on tight, brother Fidel, this is hell's own party, and remember that any fucker who gives in is a son of the devil himself.

OK bros up the scaffold with everything at first light yes sir get up stupid you and Alonso are old hands don't answer to me like that I'll strip your asshole nitwit fucker this is what the basket guy said the pig is bald anyone afraid should leave the fright at home the one that comes here needs to have great big balls this platform is not right oh yes maybe your fucked-up mother came to place it don't act important the one that thinks he's boss maybe is a Pachuco maybe that's why he talks that way well maybe he's babies' auntie but he's more vulgar than his feet if he gets nasty with you remind him of his mother right away brother how could I do that? uh you're stupid they drove you down from the mountain hitting you on the head with a hat tell him to go and fuck his mother inside a container with lime so the old lady would peel all over the place the more you take from him the more he gives it to you he's not a bad stiff actually maybe badly inflated several've given him their ass but it is the same as if someone touches his ass when he's sleeping he really takes heavy teasing yes but what about when Beibón gets him even his little hole shrinks Beibón is the only one to put him in his place with him he gets butterflies in the guts that happens to anyone with Beibón did I tell you about him? Yes it's better for you to know about it so you'll be careful with him because Beibón is death itself disguised as an innocent boy come on don't exaggerate Beibón is that short one with the brushlike hair look at him he's real dark one of his legs is kind of lame and shorter than the other but his arms are very strong when he gets mad he's the devil smiles like a little boy his face has fine features but he's a screwed-up little angel that fucker fights only when he's drunk that's when the others all come down on him and he repays with interest anyone near him no matter how insignificant what happens is well you're stupid learn how to speak the lingo or everyone is going to make fun of you here with the Raza it doesn't sound right to say yes mister at your service in a nice way and that's the way the hot weather is shit! if you want these guys to respect you you've got to say that your asshole is backwards because of so much fucking heat no you teach me how to give birth and educate children OK! don't get mad don't piss on me you when you grab my prick but that's all over now go on with the Beibón now if you're mad well suck me bad and if you don't dig it go frig it go quick and suck my dick you'll see how much it makes you pee shit! you're talk is no longer than Chicorriatas's hose not even a fucking cat jumps as good as the gimp he's so light he doesn't come down hard that's why he carries the steel blade and he knows how to use it I want you to know it and even worse one day we had some drinks in La Matanza bar a stupid jerk called him peg leg fucking Chueco started jumping like a mountain lion with Christian skin the other guy strong as a bull tried to slam him with several fucking blows but nothing but air ah but that sonofabitch Chueco got him next to the navel with the blade lousy creep don't you know who castrated the Apaches OK let me go you pup and in a jiff I'll be alert and you'll do to me like the wind did to Juárez whose cap only weighed him down and me a little bit more but without harming my chicks now you're on your way like they say friend and so and the guy goes out fucking fast yelling for someone to stop the squirting ketchup later he came with his brother who was sleeping at home get up! wake up brother

I got into a fight quick pass me the grass and come and help me to smash his mouth fucking man he was about six-three Kung Fu they said he got the Chueco cornered and kicked his ass front and back got him all red with blood sonofabitch all sure of himself so give me every fucking brownie shorty in the place to come down on prick like a plane Kung Fu went after Beibón fucking shouting knocking his ears no the peg leg calmed him down with a broad blade knife flap! blood shit guts lots of it after a week he got out of jail self-defense they called it as Cerveza said when he killed the turkeys I told Beibón don't go around like an old lady claiming you shoved it in up to the handle moving the blade cutting guts that's fine from that day on he didn't say a thing about it but even then he came near me with a grin and softly said you know that's the third one I iced the first one I threw in the river they haven't found him yet and as Don Teofilito said they won't find him I won't tell you about the second one because he was a lawman and as for the last one well same thing but different listen bro I'm tired of hearing about your rowdiness here for the most part we're decent folk well if you talk about sweet things then you'll put everyone to sleep and why's there so much violence in my church Chente tell this guy why there's so much fucking around well bro the Raza gets that way when there is no hope of being anything but a beggar and a slave you just get tired and with no hope your life is nothing what kind of respect are you talking about many of these guys are poor bastards with the family and the children at night they're something else some screwing and then sleep straight through this stuff kills the weak if someone gives up because it's too hard the other guys say that he gave his bare ass that's why it's better to protect yourself and take the violence no not all of them are that way look over there that gorilla he never says a thing he only laughs and on Fridays he changes his money in the bar together with everybody else and faster than a flash he goes home and nobody says that his ass smells because he can wipe their face with a fucking blow pay attention bro that guy with the patches on his face that's Dog every Monday he comes late to work with his face all bloody puffed up from fighting just look at him he's missing half an ear it was bitten off by another guy he doesn't even know his name if you introduce him to another bastard he says I'm Dog at your service among the approximately fifty here there are some more or less educated they talk to you like apostles a few are awful and they just waste their time you know don't call them by name because they'll cuss you out like a duel and the words have to rhyme and they have to take it without getting mad it's a great game but a red-hot one after playing it the guys are left boiling mad but if anyone shows it and starts a fight well word gets around and no one plays with him anymore they break the rule and shout so they can be heard the elevator rumbles together with the cement mixing machines and the carpenters hammering the motors lifting the loads the foremen's hysterical voices things that fall down lots of sweat and still these guys with their fooling around it doesn't matter if you tell them in good faith pay attention they'll kick you out for no reason at all hey bro! the only beard you have is the one around your asshole and that's all you want it's sure something when they throw really bad lines at each other be careful church-going man because life is not sold by contraband traders see how Manuel and Chacho ended up by taking out their blades to cut each other's guts out right there in La Matanza bar if it wasn't because Chueco el Mocho told them to cool it and not to fool around when they can't take it like men shut your traps and go fight like faggots so they shook hands and apologized and here I am going backwards in time to tell how it really was Manuel shouted hey Chango! I bounce my balls against you Chacho said then I'll nail them Manuel says you and who else and I'll stick it to you good if else doesn't like it he answered get your ass over here real slow like so I can do it right then Chacho went on and on and left Manuel red as a beet and like nothing like that he spoke right back a donkey stuck his thing in a pretty cup and your fucking mother's mouth was watering now tell me where is it Sonora or Arandas Manuelito's a faggot ass Manuel took off with the first thing and there go some real great lines don't live in the chalet where you gave me a blow job now I hang out in the cavern your mother gives me who shit you cut Chacho big ass motherfucker faggot's asshole and then Chacho says my father was a gentleman my mother a fine lady you're the spawn of a dog and your fucking mother's a streetwalker it doesn't count it doesn't count because the last line didn't really rhyme maybe it didn't but it's true you son of a bitch these fights are what leave the old folks alone and without sons well poor people have the right to have fun too you know.

We've just gotten back from another day's work harder and rougher than the last because of the decline in your ability to handle it and in your spirit. Brother Fidel almost used up all his energy. Yet he doesn't refuse to talk, and he likes to discuss things, and even though he pretends that certain topics surprise him, he's the one to bring them up. Deep down he's got a good sense of humor. The climate that envelops us is like a torturous luminosity. As for me, I have a rare gift that's somewhat complex. The fact is that in effect I inhabit several planes simultaneously, perhaps because with a biting rebelliousness I refuse to adhere to the localist dictates referring to the concept of time, which invalidate for us a multiple dynamic and project us along a single dimension, against the power of free and ubiquitous spirit and thought. I am presently occupied with two arduous daytime tasks, each one in a very different context, not to mention the family life in which my presence is also a factor. At night I write by hand while, alien to literature, I wander among past experiences. In this way, from the past, without ignoring tangible realities, I project myself into the future, whether from strength or because whimsy requires it. I'm on the edge of collapse at this point. One's energies often have narrow confines, by contrast to the boundless ones in which one's will is situated and this is even more so when sleep disappears in this already extended period of time. But in the end, calm will return free of routines. . . .

Once again, the she burro returns to the wheat. You've spent another sleepless night. Good morning, Mr. Owl. You're going to end up dead rather than asleep. You've gone too far this time. Holy Roller Brother, I've only got ten weeks to finish this book and send it off to some professors in Mexico for a contest at some remote university. It's a real nice literary contest with a neat name: Literarycosmos. Good grief, even if what you are about is an unending parade of stupidities and you go on and on about strange things, which are at times even gross, I really feel sorry for you, because you've got something more than a screw loose. But, what are you doing, you dope, you're tearing up what you wrote. I reread it, brother, and it's probably OK as a beginner's attempt concerning the Spanish language and its history here in these parts, but it ends up sounding more whining in tone than is necessary, thirteen pages in which the topic won out over my intelligence. I, as a simple referee who needs to be impartial, have decreed that these pages are going into the garbage. As far as formulas are concerned not even the narrator gets off free, and this sounds to me like something close to demagogy. It's not possible to fix the world with ideas and preaching. Excuse me, but it's better to provide images, testimonies that are more or less faithful to human events, so everyone can come to his own conclusions on the basis of what works for him as example and teaching. If a story is on target about realities and hidden motives, it will serve as a mirror and an entertainment for whoever reads it. He might be the night watchman, brother scribe, but in all this gossip mongering, what profit is there for writers or for you with all the painful years you've worked at this with nothing to show for it. And don't even think about telling me that there are satisfactions, because you always end up resentful of yourself and you keep right on enslaved to your own stupidity. You should be a minister in my church, but first you'd have to wash your mouth out with a lot of soap and singe that mouth of yours that has nothing but filthy things to say. Fidelito, this activity is pursued with passion, which is how the soul moves among the flames, paying its way with unpleasantness and deception. The possession of gold usually goes beyond everything that is desirable, but not other values to which the centuries themselves bow down. Well, my fine fool of a writer, if you are talking about things of faith, I believe you. But tell me, cotton head, do you get something from all this, anything, during the course of your lifetime. OK, I'll show you without gypsy tricks, tricks which leave no room for even the smallest amount of doubt: I will publish more than ten books, I will become a professor in important universities, I will receive honorary doctorates and prestigious literary prizes, I will make fun of the dwarves who feed on envy. So, what do you think, Holy Roller brother. Well, just to hear you going on about such pipe dreams gets my goat. Before your brain goes out on you completely, I want you to listen to me and . . . And who gives you the right to talk so blithely about the future, you blasphemer. It's just that if I'm not a real author, I at least have the spark that God gives every creative person: the spark of intuition. That's what let's you guess? More or less. In literary creation, the earthly concept of time has no meaning and past, present, and future occupy a single dimension, which the fluid person can nonetheless discern by the effects of contemplation and much reflection. Only God has that power, you high-and-mighty man. You should know, you two-bit theologian, that God does not think. How can you claim that, you fool. He doesn't need to think, because he's all intuition. He knows everything from a glance, and he doesn't think because he has no doubts to clear up, and he has no need to work things out. He's constantly intuiting things so he can be creating universes and everything that exists. Up there in heaven, you can see in the stars the traces of his grandiose creation, and down here his handiwork is in the rivers, the mountains, and the seas. He's given us a small spark of grace and we true artists are like miniature gods. You really surprise and anger me and what you're saying really burns me up. Well, if you know so much about the future, just tell me, do you know what will become of my life? Will I become a doctor of bodies and souls? A brilliant theologian? Will they build statues to honor my fame? Hee, hee, hee. Come on, tell me, what will happen to my family, to me, I'm going along with you, because I'm not about to pay for your predictions, I'm listening. OK. Let me see, you're twenty-three. . . . You've been married five years. . . . Four children . . . Seven plus twenty-five. That's it! Do you really love your wife, Fidelito? A whole lot, she's the love of my life. I adore her because she's good and she's pretty, she's a God-fearing Christian like I am, and I owe the good fortune of her company to him. Do you love your children? With all my soul, as Our Lord loves us. Well then consider what your life and the life of your children will be like: in thirty-two years, you will abandon your wife because she has gotten old, ugly, sick, and all wrinkled. Shut up, you crazy liar! Nor will you ever see your children and your grandchildren again. You will give up everything for a beautiful and sensuous twenty-year-old who will be better in bed than the Queen of Sheba. What a stupid thing to say! You and she will emigrate to a faraway island. There, after a few years, you will die all alone, with your eyes all dried up, devoid of tears. How can you insult me in this way. You've no right to. Ask my forgiveness for saying these horrible things to me, you tin-plate writer. I can't, dear friend, because it's done. Why do you assert such a thing with so much confidence? Because I know it. I'm narrating things retrospectively, you dunce!, from the point of view of 1991. Nevertheless, Fidel, you and I are now navigating these pages, on a construction site, during this fictitious year of 1953. I don't understand any of your madness and I don't want you to infect me. You're taking advantage of how I can't understand any of this business about agricultures, literatours, and retrosectives, and I don't know what the heck other looniness just to confuse me. Ah, the bad part is going to happen to me and you're going to get off with only roses. Just give time its due, little brother, and I'll get around to telling you about the tragic side of my life in an, in the main, autobiographical novel that I'm already making notes for. I don't want to hear your jokes from the devil again. I won't tell you anything else, so let's get going to the construction site. Since we're new with this construction company, in only four days we know little about these people we're working with and so we've got to get to know them better, don't you think? You like wild people better than living in the holy peace of God, whose humble servant I am.

OK fellows let's hit it hard yes sir be careful man you might fall down listen buddy I'm going to tell you about the life concerning those kids on the move what do you know about that heh heh hee hee hee the devil knows what he knows because he's old not because he's the devil the devil can't even get to third base you talk funny like they do where I come from hey you're kind of old to be mixed up in this kind of work the first time you get dehydrated you'll kick the bucket all these statues are kid stuff for me like here it's hard you really bust your balls working like this just like an animal anybody can turn his guts inside out these guys get their kicks pulling off things like hoods because that's all they have to do any kind of sport costs them too much they even have fun hurling gross insults at each other what the fuck they build mansions every day and live in shitty huts look watch your mouth I see something in your eyes your expression as though I know you from way back how old are you old-timer I'm as old as you are sixty-two come on I'm only twenty-three I was born in 1930 what's going on huh you don't bathe well then take care of yourself with those people an old man's talking to you I can't remember you old man I can see you look like me a half-thousand miles away bronco Pachuco pocho and college graduate when you comb your hair you know what happened last week when our Holy Roller friend Fidelito and you hadn't shown up yet and note I say "our" friend because I like Fidel Castillo how did you know his last name I heard it man the way you ask questions and you see me opening my eyes wide as though I didn't trust you I talk any way I want that's for sure according to the situation or the occasion but not to the extent you do because you're all fired up over what you're doing what are you talking about old man what and how do you know about what I'm doing? don't interrupt me and let me talk fuck it here we are in the middle of the desert well those creeps who're cleaning out the underbrush ahead of us run into rattlesnakes every day one of those cocksuckers tossed a rattler at us down there Chicorriatas grabbed it and half-stunned it with a club then he tossed it inside the box of the cement mix going up on the elevator for the use of the masons the snake was good and alive and mad as hell the guys who divide up the mix one of them hid it part way in the trough of the one who's a mastodon that gringo they call Litter Joe because he bends over to grab from the can he stirs the mixture as usual with the ladle and then he lifts that honcho snake part way out and he's sticking his tongue out you and that joker jump back like he's been hit by lightning then they served it up to that black guy Sam who's always talking and laughing real loud and waving his hands around he went to move the mixing board because Chicorriatas asked him to he challenged him by saying you're stronger than Superman and they're fanning whitey with a hat when he picked the plank up grabbing it by both ends with his extralong arms, that damned snake stretched himself out and give a great big kiss to the black guy who barely had time to yell and to fling the thing away taking off like a bat out of hell and raising such a ruckus that it sounded like the uproar of a dozen terrified banshees and then the Pachuco who was the foreman came up with the engineer in charge Mr. Adams like he didn't know what was going on and planted himself right next to the snake it's a good thing he was wearing boots they saved him because the infuriated serpent bit the cuff of his pant leg he shook him lose making such an uproar he looked like an old lady he whacked him one with the level and then killed him by smashing his head I think there must have been some baby snakes because it continued to twist about Chicorriatas grabbed it by the tail and went down the elevator he said to throw it away and that's just when the real pretty little white girl shows up with her meal cart that's right one of those wagons with sides that open up so you can sell hot food she said OK you drunkards it's chow time you should see how they grab tacos sandwiches meat bean burros hotdogs and whatever their guts clamor for she laughs like a real tease she wears those shorts that climb up the ass she takes in even the ugliest man of the bunch what can I tell you they're all the same that son of a bitch Chicorriatas tied the snake as tight as he could around the handlebars of the traveling lunchroom when all of the workers were on their way back to their jobs Marlene who knows where her mind was climbed aboard her provocative wagon waving and showing off to her customers and admirers get a load of her she felt something soft on the steering wheel tried to jump down and fell scared out of her wits there's the villain of the piece hot on her tail and who else would it be but the devil himself Chicorriatas thrust an arm between her legs with the other around her neck he dragged her to a shady spot between all the workers they collected two hundred dollars at two dollars a head hiccuping and sobbing she grabbed the money with a little laugh and then ran off to do her business that SOB Chicorriatas couldn't help himself with so much glory and started to blab about when he stuck his hand down inside her blouse he grabbed one of her naked boobs and he claimed he also felt her you know where he made everybody laugh about how when he lifted her up she peed herself and let some farts go like when Pancho Villa entered Torreón with his machine gun firing Chicorriatas disappeared who knows where the matter about the snakes didn't stop there the tractor devils frequently toss two or three in the carts when it's time to knock off we all try to catch a glimpse just in case more than four have shit their pants when they hear the rattlers under their seats or in front of them why are you staring at me so pensively well didn't you like the story yes . . . you make the story sound interesting . . . someone . . . I don't know who I have the idea he told me about it with the very same words and gestures I'd say a while back I don't know how since it's only been about eight days look old man I can't believe it come on what's your name tell me your complete name ah fuck it Simón Pelagallos is calling me I'll be right there look Chente what's the name of that old timer who the fuck knows the only thing I know is that everybody calls him the old timer a little while ago the foreman himself asked "listen guys who's the dude who brought that fucking kid around just so he could rush him off to his house" damn it! the kid fades in my mind and his face doesn't come to me I want to ask him how many dogs there are in the gallows and nothing let me get him I'll be back Chatunga I'm going to the bathroom that brother don't go to the hole throne or the potty anyway you want it hey we're raising walls on the four sides don't you know well the hole is right in the middle anyone that goes in gets it the Raza starts throwing bricks on the little room the other day I went to throw some crap well right away the bombs started falling on the thin roof on the side boards I was scared bad better wait a little while when the chiefs are here nobody can bother you because they might get caught and punished no better do it in your pants doesn't matter if you smell like a dead cat I'm telling you this because you're a good guy be alert man like you were mounting on a mule don't fall down since it's Friday payday when the eagle shits we'll go to the La Matanza to cash our checks and on the way we'll drink some cool ones brother there you can get a ride with the guys you know that I don't go to La Matanza don't sweat it Fidelito I'll catch up with you after La Matanza we'll get a bite somewhere it's dark now time to get some sleep listen old man you're going to La Matanza naturally my man to have a talk with you about who I am and who you were if this old guy's not the devil in person who do you think he is ask them to serve a little pregnant one and whoever says no is a dark dog's ass hole yep he's the one all right yes a pregnant one it's a big bottle of beer with a small cup of tequila well I want a pregnant one with my friends the Pachuco knows his business he speaks English just like Lolo he pretends to be stupid just to get along with the guys what's happening you look sad what's up now he doesn't have a fuck of a thing to say you always arguing now there you're dragging your face on the ground I'm kind of sick also real tired out I'm having trouble sleeping truth is that half the feathers are gone from my wing and I'm so tired it looks like twice the amount well try not to worry brother just look at your eyes they look like plastic half-moons what's worse is that these drinks are coming one after the other I'm seeing double like things suspended in air like everything flying around me and at the same time everyone's talking all at once in a single shrieking well have yourself another so it'll go away you know what boys I'm going to go have a chat with the old man I think I know him what are you laughing about old man about our bad deeds it's a cinch I was waiting for you what can you tell me about Che your brother what do you mean Che my brother where'd you get that you know what is none of your business listen old man it's not just because I've had some drinks hear me out I want you to know that I'm in charge of everything around here and here you are out of control you ask me things I'm not putting into your mouth I know . . . come over here and get a good look at me I bet you don't know me I'm from down Sinaloa way I called you wild Yaqui Indian you called me Culi . . . Culichi? Cruz Ramos! Cruz, is that you? hey what's going on here listen I'm the one who's come back here to try to reconstruct the atmosphere of the 1950s it's a calling that distracts me then I want to recall what Mexicans were like back then how they talked how they thought how they lived everything that concerns us so we can be whole so the new ones will understand the mark we've been leaving you see everything is quickly erased if we heed the wind to leave a trace on things that should not be forgotten yes yes OK OK you go on writing we were doing it back then besides you get yourself all fucked up with dumb things like that that suck all the juices from you handling heavy materials like it was some kind of race and protecting yourself from knocking your brains out high up there then your academic plane your students come on don't get it all screwed up pace your energies and Cruz how did you get to know something like that bah gossip is like birds on the wing who go and sing their song all over the place besides I'm just one step away from another dimension where no one not even the writers know a single thing aside from meaningless speculations here let me tell you Cruz I don't know if this is true it's been one night after the other since I last slept all I do is write out of a determination to complete this literary tour in time aside from the cattle runs under the burning sun well also the hardship of working on that other level that you commented on I'm all worn out with a fever that's pounding right down into the marrow of my bones and I'm a little upset with all these drinks no you can't be here through your own will I'm seeing visions it's not possible for me to be hearing you say this my mind is wandering no no a writer of the sands is inside out it's me the big cheese himself whose mind is wandering I'm giving my last gasps I'm dying this very minute down in Mazatlán if you want to know I'll be frank if I don't sneak here into your private cosmos it would be impossible when I started really raving my head off is when I come across your little joke you really mean it?! what am I seeing look they're my fellow workers from long ago how pretty! and I join the gang carrying bricks I recognized all of them and not one jerk recognized me since I just came in illegally and not backside first without your permission look at me here with the same skeleton of a sixty-year-old man making fun of your writing and your belief that you're a big deal right now I'm surrounded by my children and my old woman back there at home well I think I died something happened the fact is that I hollered and that scared the daylights out of Venustiana and I fall into a delirium a real fucking strange one as though I was walking in a forest of humongous trees but they're all dried out without a single damn leaf on them not even one you could make a cup of tea from where the hell are me and the horse well hurry up! these vegetables are shaped like letters but really very bad ones hey get a load of who the fuck wrote this the letter *T* yuck like crosses in the cemetery better knock on wood capital *B* like the naked buns of Miss Buck Naked Miami Acapulco you're the very same Cruz Ramos a card to the very end if I didn't know you were dying I would give you a good kick in the butt ay and what you wouldn't give me let's see if right now I'm a . . . a what . . . a dumb jerk you're the dumb jerk if this is a, so to speak, an oneiric dream in a fictitious literary text yes I know I'm a spoutuspiritual being you're still the same Culichi you're still the same I noticed that the trees were lined up in ditches I set about reading them I found out about Fidel the gang he fell in with the whole story about his death no! if I were to tell you that two boobs pull stronger than two tractors and short and curly hair from down there more than a train you poor little Holy Roller suddenly I'm right there among you making you talk nonsense like you do to Fidel poor Culichi your family must be suffering a lot because it's a little bit of pain a lot of theater they're tearing their hair out weeping and wailing over a few skinny cows that look like amazons with corners on them and all sorts of goings on that aren't worth aspirins taken for flying off the handle ask that Holy Roller Fidel if he remembers the fifty dollars I lent him I collected it from him who the hell knows how many times and he would turn to the Bible I'm falling asleep cross myself my eyes are closing on me I'm falling asleep that's not worth a shit I'm dying my soul is barely hanging on by a thread you must've noticed that every now and then I dash off to pee no really I'm sure I'm on my way out just so I don't go without some kind of joke that really makes me laugh keep in mind that you're seeing me give my last gasps right at this very motherfucking moment stuck back in a room in my house my children and the old woman with tear-stained faces sunken eyes just a little bit sad wishing more for me to pop off instead of struggling day in and day out my friends and relatives waiting outside the door with their ears cocked to see if I die what the hell is he waiting for well he was a great man Culichi doing coffee with sugarcane alcohol he's going to sprout mushrooms while here I am lost in the middle of your writing like someone who's crashed the party don't tell me with your permission not on your ass hah hah hah how I like pork urine hah hah hah how you doing dying there Cruz but that doesn't keep you from having a big mouth dirty mouth ah now we've really gone and done it that's the way I talk and I've never stolen anything from anybody nor have I killed anyone nor poisoned any addicts a very good man I've been that's why I'm dying happy poor saps who talk real pretty and then get all scared when they hear ay a swearword well just look at that a lot of them not all of them are lousy thieving criminals a shit-filled sewer hole fucking cocksuckers when you sleep or I kick off forever for your information Beibón's number came up in California in 1980 they put a bullet through his head like they do to pigs in the slaughterhouse Dog is still dragging his butt all over the place a bunch of those who are bad off thanks to your pack of fucking lies it's a hell of a situation you won't believe it but Chicorriatas went and married that little blonde thing who sold little toys all those children of your fantasies look at them dancing like circus clowns to the music of jukeboxes they're spastic more than one of them with more rheumatism than kisses their grandmother gave them Fernando el Chípili died sitting on the sofa chatting with his old lady answer me Fernando you distracted old man talk to me you fool . . . I dash off because I'm about to pee OK little bed put it into drive toward home it's going on and on I'm your buddy Beibón the good bowed one hey let's go in Hare's old jalopy here is your ole pal Goat Reyes we'll be home in a jiffy we're taking him because he's a neat guy a little mysterious brother sometimes we watch him talking to himself pensively quite a little devil but not mean at all he makes us walk with him OK we give him a hand so he can walk without falling flat on his face OK buddy we're almost home now so Fidelitooo here's your pal a little on the other side OK Fidel yes you put it there we'll see you at dawn hey what do you have there uuh you're progressing Writerbert says you're sure coming well served but you've really got a high fever you'll have to go see the sawbones a hot cup of coffee with aspirins meantime you should've seen Fidelito what a lovely gesture the students showed up in the morning in class with their eyes shining and with enormous pleasure they told me bursting with pride congratulations professor you're so Mexican it's wonderful Octavio Paz has just been given the Nobel Prize for Literature the Chicanos hugged me filled with joy well done professor well done they hugged each other and shook hands among themselves brother you're really sick going on deliriously about such stupid and strange things dumb things you pick up from those useless books you read if you read the Good Book these things wouldn't happen to you Fidelito don't be silly pay your fifty dollars to Culichi Cruz Ramos I haven't paid him because I haven't seen him where'd you see him how'd you know I owed him money I want you to know brother just to make you mad and don't tell me I talk too much another hot shit writer among the hot shits also a Nobel Prize winner a man with really big balls visited me seems like yesterday Don Camilo José Cela my good friend Don Camilo I'm just a peasant from Sonora man! I'm a peasant from Galicia take two more aspirins and get some sleep you're talking now about people who don't exist and things that never happened I feel sorry for you I already told you you've got a screw loose and it's gotten so bad you've lost the screw brother in Christ Fidel I want to say good-bye to you may God forgive us both so much pride may your soul be at peace God is magnanimous by the skin of a chicken's tooth I almost ended up lost among these landscapes of the past only because of that old man who is getting on everybody's business and who wanted me to go along with him Culichi well fellow you're nuts if you think Cruz Ramos is a young man dawn won't find us here tomorrow Fidelito you're going to end up in Hawaii in a small town of very silent people that's called Necropolis there you'll be real quiet no one'll try your patience there'll be no dirty thoughts to give you a case of galloping Solomonitis let's take a thirty-eight-year leap I'm going to change into an old professor without any hair half-blind with the force of gravity obliging him to walk looking down at the ground yes man yes whatever you say but shut up now and sleep you stubborn drunk farewell brother what the heck what a crazy nut you turned out to be but who cares so long as you get some rest shut your trap and let's see if you can get over that fever otherwise you're not going to be able to . . . so long . . .

"**I refuse** to dictate an ending that will make this text circular, one whose ends and development are meant to imitate unpredictable fate in the way in which it is chaotic, like so much of life that happens without being touched up by some imaginative tyrant just because he's got the vain idea that he is omniscient. Nevertheless, because I am arbitrary like every pretentious person who sets out to shatter convention because it is obsolete, in exchange for uncertain revitalizations that could well turn out more counterproductive than anything else, I have forged this story bearing in mind as a model the specter of a river of letters and words in widening currents of jargon, slang, dialects, hybrid and foreign voices, in swirling linguistic colloquialisms that make up, express languages that are evolving, turning revolutionary, and therefore metamorphic to a large degree. An overflowing river of letters and words that can never be contained.

"Certainly, the most varied means of communication are highly effective, but the demographic phenomenon that alters spaces and times are the determining factors for bringing about these vertiginous changes that end up being chaotic for those academics who have lost sight of the onomatopoeia of languages, children of the basest and what's worse, bastard, terminology. Yes, a river of letters into which linguistic streams and even tributaries flow dynamically, to the point of madness. And yet are not the numerous volumes that swell the already overflowing rivers captivating because they are contemplatable, in the sense of engulfing everything and imposing new realities, like any phenomenon that keeps a world from being static, in spite of whatever anyone might think or want?

"Thus, elitist groups, which are smaller and smaller every day in relation to the boundless expansion of the masses, are by apparent coincidence the bearers of prestige, power, and wealth. The masses, in open growth and by contrast the lords and masters of poverty, have been given as a natural gift and mysterious grace the rare privilege that consists of nullifying the effect of languages to the point of their extinction and, in fact, of giving form to new ones with the invention of terms, the alteration of words and archaic structures, the acquisition of foreign phrases and the ones that spring from alien terms in free exchange among themselves, as well as other undetectable reasons. Might these not be the same mechanisms to be found in the collective soul of people, which via the effect of some sort of interior reaction, turn thanks to this phenomenon into vengeance in the face of unimagined cynicism, lies, and injustice? If it were thus, then let it be said that good speech, channeled by precepts and wise academic rules, requires, in order to reaffirm the solidity and the glory of a language, that the little man be respected and dignified, since his imagination and nature are also a reflection of the Almighty Creator."

Around about February and from Mallorca an island off Spain and ensconced in the belly of mechanical birds a unique gentleman is traveling toward Tucson, an Arizonan city crimeney the telephone is ringing who's calling at this hour it's Camilo José Cela don't say how are you it's a pleasure for me to be talking to you I want to go to Tucson to observe that world do come we'll be expecting you he crossed the sea mountains clouds cities rivers deserts a writer who walks notices observes learns on the go despite his experience wisdom talent I'm doing it so I won't make too many mistakes I'm seeking background verisimilitude my novel in progress Christ versus Arizona it will be located in these parts he asks questions takes notes thinks invents creates publishes books profoundly revealing books bitter poetic erudite they teach move tie things together entertain hurt C.J.C. experiments with themes renews spaces revolutionizes techniques occupies a privileged place among the most brilliant writers welcome to Tucson Maestro Camilo José Cela I had a busy day in Miami lecture and banquet I'm happy we'll get your luggage then to the hotel tomorrow an outing and a long talk a man of many places and maritime navigation a traveler through Alcarria a vagabond from Miño to Bidasoa welcome to these lands in light and dark dawn bordering the dunes of the Sonoran Desert the empire of that king His Majesty the Saguaro I feel like I'm going to be dizzy it's nothing but no sir political struggle and literature are not synonyms literary art and talent are something else the marriage of two-bit politicians only produces books to fill the kiosks of the Indians of this Tucsonian region I would say that the Papagos are the natives they've recently decided to call themselves Tohono Oodjans so you can see they're part of the Pima family basically peaceful by nature the mission founded by Father Eusebio Kino is located in the area designated for them it goes by the name San Javier Mission and it has the poetic title of The Dove of the Desert the Papago women weave baskets while at the same time they transmit to their children cultural matters that are their guardians by means of anecdotes canticles and stories hungry and thirsty Apaches can be found wandering these sunstroke-inducing lands they sought peace and food while leaving behind a wake of the weak the wounded or those in the process of spilling their life along with the very blood of Cochise and Geronimo what a story what terrible fame what men the bald truth is that these guys are now pure folklore legends movies and such and thousands of Yaquis live now in Tucson in exodus they arrived at the dawn of this century the history of these people would make the sons of ancient Spartacus shit their pants what a tough people what a warlike people Diego de Guzmán must have been telling it to the devil when he landed in the fires of hell itself in the 1930s they signed a pact with the government of Mexico after four hundred years of struggle they never gave themselves up to Spain in the first place they fought like hell and they held the Spanish soldiers off even if at the end of the seventeenth century they accepted the Jesuits the meaning of the word Yaqui really means a man who speaks with strength and that's no accident hey watch out one day we'll talk about these guys there's no such thing as good and bad words only your intention and good or bad understanding for example for you to say crap without being embarrassed but if on the other hand you hear asshole you turn all red say instead that asshole is where the nobility of the spinal column ends call it a noble part or better your privates when the asshole includes surrounding accessories around here Maestro the populace defines the concept of the asshole in a no-nonsense fashion well go ahead and tell me what they say they say that the asshole is where the hide swirls how pretty how pretty let me write that down look Camilo José that obese thing is a barrel cactus it looks like a barrel decked out with knives it's pulp is soft like that of all the cactuses it really looks like a big-bellied camp follower attached to one of those peasants in big sombreros who fought alongside General Zapata his chlorophylled humanity crisscrossed with cartridge belts with spines in their slots as though they were bullets you can't imagine how hard it is to kill someone from Galicia if perhaps you are able to kill one of them don't be surprised if he keeps on living like that Galician they killed while he was sleeping and when he woke up can you imagine he was already dead you are intrigued by the ocotillo that cluster of long thin green arms whose trunk lies underground in the spring its tips are bloody with phosphorescent flowers to the delight of traveling butterflies and hummingbirds that fly about the paths and byways seeking the never seen to pluck the beauty of what is made only once they look and look and remember it Did you take a picture of the palo verde? as long as it doesn't die it stays permanently green the ironwood is a unique tree its chucks of wood weigh as much as iron when it's made into firewood it'll ruin the solidest of metals it burns so hot that women who are like it are called ironwood-burning ovens the Castilian spoken here by the Indians is always sonorous always living the echoes of silence speak an entire world when they look be careful Camilo José you see how that Siviri cactus wields its knife blades its name is Yaqui if you get too close to it it jumps and your hide ends up like a pin cushion without your even touching it it'll attack you according to a legend about tequila-drinking cowboys the Spanish language transforms itself into so many bastardized words along the frontier from white and dark languages and faces we say *buqui* for child *juila* for bicycle *pinche vato* for someone who's stupid and so many other words that are even more barbarous that you members of the Royal Academy would say man that doesn't have anything to do with it language is like an impetuous river we ephemeral beings are only its banks so it will survive it's its nature to move and flow among forests of weeks mountains deserts and even seas of years those poor vain individuals who might attempt to contain it because more than lakes they would create vile stagnant pools understand that this does not occur in five decades nor is it a question of tossing speech overboard as a gesture of absurd libertinism long live literature sirs you also said in the lecture you gave at the University of Arizona on 23 February 1987 between four and six in the afternoon may these facts serve for posterity to take notice but how important the saguaros are in this world of scarce and determined vegetation look at those giants how they rise up their insides are overflowing with water here where the clouds are only doves that fade away among blue dust storms forgive this one that moistened its little wings in your flesh they are so firm so tall and proud look how they cover that leveled-off mountain that looks like a wall of intercalated rock from over there from its sharp-nosed peak down to this snake-filled gully that snaps at its feet who could imagine the vast wall of rock is filled with a multitude of the green titans where they put down their roots where they sink their claws in now let's take a close-up look at the saguaros they look like the columns of a Greek temple they're a dark green in times of drought and an intense green when it rains the sap covers the pulp they're soft despite their consistency from one end to the other they are marked by parallel ribs with an armor of long thorns like the nails of elegant women they use them to wound the flesh without so much as a by-your-leave of incautious people who go up and touch them the arms of the saguaros give them the most capricious shapes that produce varied and multiple images and seem to be like shy men or ones who are completely naked with their sex erect or women who watch over their vassals or engender them out in the open without anyone thinking to accuse them of being obscene or immoral some are more than seventy feet tall and more than two hundred years old nature gave them the power to be so many gigantic vegetables as well as to be a living statuary of the existence of beings sculpted like animated monuments Loli this tastes real good very delicious what a pretty young lady Isabel Cristina is look at how graceful she is right Miguel in the full bloom of her sixteen years attractive right Maestro the publishers have pocketed my royalties they confiscate my books nevertheless the things I write have helped me indirectly what are you complaining about man you have a nice home a darling family when I published *The Family of Pascual Duarte* I only received 1,500 pesetas for three printings it's the same everywhere I spent five years on *The Hive* I wrote *Trip to the Alcarria* in a week the photographers and the journalists are a plague with their articles when Pío Baroja died they said that Hemingway carried his coffin on his shoulders three friends and I carried the bier to the hearse Hemingway was on the sidelines bawling like an old lady that dense undergrowth of a sickly green carpet broad plains cast your glance over there where the confines with their ashen snouts overwhelm the view well you should know that that bush is called stinkweed and it's often also called governess for its intense bad odor it tolerates vegetables of other species throughout the domains where it has spread its shade it's a pleasure to be your friend Don Camilo to call you Maestro and to hear you talk about profound things penetrating events and an anecdote now and then tinged with irony perhaps so as not to fall into sentimentality let's leave melancholy to foolish old women Camilo friend let them wail over the past and wet their pants in their nostalgia I think I'm going to be sick now a glass of bacanora it's very strong careful you were telling me about Oteliña a queen of Sheba ah yes a very good woman svelte and wise well with a woman driver like that I'm not talking about the Alcarria one wandered aimlessly around there on more than one occasion with my guts mere ornaments on foot covering my sleep with the stars feeding themselves on notes forty years later in a Rolls Royce musical accompaniment and a charming and pretty black driver as much wine and food as I could want sleep at night and afternoon naps how pretty how pretty better than a party among penguins I got affection from the hands of people and recognition from mayors and that's the best prize bah there's no better treasure well let's go rest we need to tomorrow we'll go on another outing look how long that photographer is taking a nice fellow no doubt about it I like him a lot he's noble good here he is let's get going we're almost there look at that town of Tombstone pistols bullets barricades fleshy whores bars mirrors permeated with the rust of time they suggest sheriffs Apaches Mexicans and Gringos stumbling along splintery wood-slate sidewalks the dark color of old things a people who give birth to folkloristic books a seedbed of movies about the Old West gold-seeking bandits lowlifes dreamers of a half-hidden lost beauty half floating in the air downy white tits some John Wayne-type protector who spits tobacco looks out the corner of his eyes with the air of an apostle and a famous stud the child inside you comes to the surface Camilo José just look at how you're laughing and how happy you are with this town so real and so fictional you say you would have liked to be a rustler and eat rustled beef on the open range and to fire your six-shooter right and left down these streets made for the comings and goings of drunken horsemen carriages drawn by fancy horse with a strutting gait foul-smelling men scrawny dogs with the air of gentlemen women with more petticoats than a leafy head of lettuce or a heavy onion walking along in a stiff and rolling fashion the police grabbed me after the American fashion since I was a man of crime they all had their pistols drawn this town will be where I'll place the woman of my new novel she'll be the mother of an unusual person in the pages of *Christ vs. Arizona* things will transpire adventures of considerable interest for the reader you'll see how the majority of these antimen liberationists are dykes I can tell you that I'm not convinced by the vaginocracy do you hear me well of course we men are very good and predisposed to be adored by our women just look at the two of us we're real catches what other kind of happiness do they want they must be blind I feel like I'm going to be sick the skinny coyote trots along through the fields and turns over his impossible gourmet schemes on horizons bereft of foilage he will redouble his step hours under the roasting sun his face will be all red the skyline like the blood of his feverish eyes the Mexican wolf wounds the atmosphere with his iron look the hunger he swallows contains proteins and hydrates the little horned viper snakes along the sand here among spiny bushes and cactuses they drag along a gangrenous spiral their rattlers sound they're ready to draw themselves up into a vertical flying spring its jaws open its fangs at the ready a free ride to the cemetery in a land and before a sun that are merciless in terms of that fire that whitens the sand and burns the very atmosphere to a crisp they swell with attitude they glimpse the water through their dried bladders the gnawing of hunger and thirst strip their bones and even then these beings spit toward heaven out of rage isn't there something heroic about the attitude of these beasts and animals? the roadrunner would not like to fly but if he runs around here the Indian calls him *churea* which is the name of a carnivorous bird can you imagine it fills itself up as much on lizards that snakes whether they are rattlers or nasty dudes like their mothers-in-law in the way they have of surviving they fight to the death with every type of critter just like the ancient inhabitants of Tomistón those gnawers among rats and rabbits are the *juancitos* they stick their faces out of their holes at the wayfarers just to make obscene gestures in front of them, rearing up on their hind legs well like the sun now it folds its pintail wings let's get back to Tucson don Camilo José Cela so you can have a nap and renew your goodwill we'll have dinner about 7:45 but first we'll have a drink after a beer tomorrow'll be another day and we'll go to the Grand Canyon to see that cesarean with which Father Time opened the womb of mother Earth using the scalpel of the Colorado River not to mention a huge amount of human patience good morning Maestro how're doing did you sleep well yes yes very well man let's get going eh we'll reach the big ditch in six or seven hours Maestro the novel *The Family of Pascual Duarte* is bitter wrenching and maybe even produces tears in which suffering is also a condition of our species by contrast in *Trip to the Alcarria* you'll find Cela the poet like some Machado or some José Ramón Jiménez man beauty also is to be found in *The Hive* not only does it take the pulse of Madrid but of the city no matter how well well you have it man you've got to read my *Office of Shadows* I'll send you those books and others the war hurts it was painful that was a bunch of lies while the Passionaria did not shoot Christ they say that the ballads on bullfighting are bloody and cruel if the Germans had had the running of the bulls they would have avoided a lot of bloodletting can you believe it it would be nice Maestro to institutionalize bullfights in each one of the warring powers maybe in this way poor people would not be massacred a German says that Chicano literature is the black legend of the United States now isn't that funny you're not going to tell me that History repeats itself Bartolomé de las Casas as a wetback come on! your novel the one you sent me in Spain I sent it to two respectable critics but since you're not from their whereabouts they paid no attention to it if this is what happens with great works and famous authors what can those of us who struggle to make a name for ourselves expect we've finally reached the Grand Canyon how terrifying it is to observe that slice of cataclysm as though time and the river had carved themselves on a battered landscape a great hypothesis Maestro Camilo José Cela what is most horrifying is not the precipice but the inverse spiral that runs from wide and dynamic to a narrow point diminishing and dying under the effect of dead receding time it plunges us in a regression among so very many time periods all bunched together overwhelm me dizzyingly so many petrified screams this mist that survived a genetic chaos the river in the bottom emulated some silver scalpel it plunges slices and works traces its zigzagging destiny what terrible beauty what a haughty panorama who could have lived in those mysterious castles scattered among the abysses throughout those precipices that are frightening to look at and the haughty palaces that fill one's gaze with joy who are we Camilo José who are we in what river of genes do these images travel I now fix on my retinas delving into the future from one generation to the next over millennia and millennia so that my descendants might see in that deepest gorge even greater images joined to the one I now see because I have the strange sensation of having seen this world a long long time ago through the pulverized eyes of mysterious progenitors I would like to be strong enough to unleash a cry that would penetrate time to its depths to see if I would answer myself back from there with the first shriek born of pain or pleasure someone asked a blonde one golden afternoon if the cathedrals carved by Chronos the Sculptor holding a river in his hand are of a copper red hue with a blue background that would light up in Bécquer's poetry she distractedly replied yes yes the color of copper I surely know the diction of someone who knows that love is joy and that it also wounds that monstrous cavity turned us pensive between its barbarous beauty and these atavistic self-absorptions we do not perceive the cloud that falls on us in pieces the centigrade thermometer says ten degrees below zero let's go to the hotel you suggest we've already seen this Joaquín answers let's go the mechanical crane flaps its wings or stiffens so we left the Grand Canyon looking out of the corner of our eyes and went to chow down you had a 10-ounce T-bone we had an enormous one weighing over two pounds then I caught your eloquent thought that it is possible that we Mexican Americans drink as much as people from Galicia I had a half-awake nightmare during the night that the Grand Canyon was my grave with a rainbow something like a vault the reflection of the sun with the atmosphere as a cross these are dreams of grandeur Maestro in the end any tomb is an abyss even if it's only on top of the land tomorrow we will return to Tucson for your departure right after for Spain what a white dawn what a delicious breakfast now we're heading from the Grand Canyon to Flagstaff we run into a snow storm that had been going on for eighteen hours between four thousand and fifteen hundred feet the whole thing was a Siberian spectacle in the middle of the winter we skidded for hours on an ice rink praying without realizing it we crossed mountainous hills with a short flat stretch in our descent Joaquín honk your horn when we see the first saguaro because that will be an indication that we are safe and sound yes Mister Cela I will honk the horn at the first saguaro that I see the King of desert plants is in view the horn honks and honks there's jubilation laughter praise for His Majesty the Saguaro sovereign of chlorophyll we you see here of flesh and blood glorify and greet you King Juan Carlos does not come to mind I must tell you that he's such a king and such a man that perhaps we don't deserve him he's quite an intelligent clever man the best of the best things have been a bed of roses for us I'm returning to Spain very happy thanks to you I have researched what I needed to and more Don Camilo José Cela still add to your microcosm which is already a whole universe all these things you see you will read and now I am telling you go with our affection understanding gratefulness because it's writers like you with your prolific and valuable writing who give life to the language and character to a people believe me Don Camilo José the grandeur of Spain will endure and grow with men of letters like you heck you're returning now to Spain we're in the airport now before boarding the plane so long and until we meet again your friends will remember you and miss you a great big hug Don Camilo José Cela companion in arms as you so generously call me.

My family celebrates my recovery with eloquent happiness. For the time being my body has no need for the fever. My forehead will no longer be adorned with lettuce leaves looking like Caesar crowned with laurels, much less potato skins as befitting a minor prizewinning poet. The faces of Loli, Miguelito, and Isabel show the peace and calm following intense concern. They've loudly let me know it, "Hey, great, real great, you're no longer running a fever. You've got to take care of yourself. We're not going to let you do anything foolish." I gladly laughed. Well, yes, it's true. My head recovers its freshness, quite true, and I even feel better than before. The body of hyperactive people takes advantage of periods of illness to rest and to somehow restore energy, as long as you don't end up carted off in Death's wheelbarrow to the place no one ever comes back from. Yet the confidence of my dear ones makes me laugh. They miss the point that the mental fever that afflicts me has blown the thermometer. Since I'm behind on some literary projects, my internal mechanisms and ones I have close at hand, along with the ones hidden deep in the recesses of my mind, have set their respective machineries to work in order to oblige me to channel as letters the labyrinthine excursions and other elucubrations dragging me along. Toward making a beginning I am moved, in spite of my drowsiness and lassitude, by this vocation I took on in my youth, like a virus that only gives up with the death of its victim. The term "exhaustion" does not figure in my personal lingo. But then, my taste and my will swollen, I'm a defenseless shipwreck in the infamous River of Letters, or better yet, a beggar wandering in a celestial ocean abounded in lights. If in order to travel through the physical universe dodging aerolites, plowing unforeseen spaces, not to mention other rare conditions imposed from the planets and other heavenly entities, we need ships made out of a tangible material, because you should know that in my exclusive cosmos, which is about the same size as the one the astronomers scrutinize, I'm the builder of my own vessel, whose only fuel relies on my own fantasy and storytelling powers, which are creative of course but therefore also feverish as an imperiously unavoidable condition. Without passion nothing gets created. Without fire, there would be no passion. In sum, I'm still running a fever, so what. Before my first book was published I got the idea, a little to have some fun at the expense of people around me, to say that I was a born writer. The result was like frightening pigeons and listening to them create a scandal, something like the heavy laughter that makes them take flight. Friends and immediate relatives greeted the idea with sardonic laughter and feigned pity over my madness. My girlfriend at the time demanded I shape up and act normal and assume soberly the struggle to make a place for myself in life with courage and without ridiculous chimera or harmful fantasizing. Everybody knew I had barely learned to read and write in the rural school in El Claro, but they were ignoring what they didn't know about my absolute dedication to the study of literature, much of it in hours stolen from the lethargizing influence of the night. When I published my first book back in about 1968, more than just a few people gnashed their teeth. They suddenly discovered that I wasn't the one who was foolish and that they in fact had sinned on the side of ignorance. This is no cause for celebration on the part of someone who forges his own social structure at random, situating himself in a place of privilege and leaving the rest behind at the bottom. This is my tenth book. I am working on it from my niche as a full-time professor in the Department of Romance Languages at the University of Arizona. I'm happy and I laugh at myself and the world around me. The handful of detractors I now have, a bitter critic, gratuitous envy on a minor scale all roll right off my back. Whatever the result is of this space trip dodging glowing and frozen stars, riding a space ship of my own making, ideal in its shape, I've set off on an imaginary trip that is roundabout in its action no matter how much I may think it's straight and linear in its outline. So let's see if anyone can take away from me what's already been mine. Collective amnesia, perhaps. Don Miguel de Unamuno lit a candle in universal time. Will he survive the consummation of planetary time? Poor me, I'm lighting a fleeting little taper to scare away the forgetfulness of those who have yet to be born. The cemeteries of dead memories also die in their due course. If perhaps time dies, who will give an account of space. Thus, while I meditate by giving free rein to my imagination, with no other order or law to planes and chronology that give a story symmetrical panoramas and explicit occurrences, I jump from one thing to the other on the wings of my mind. More than the attention owed to the reader and to his generous understanding, I allow myself to be carried along by the unforeseen meanderings and turnings thinking unleashes. Distant in their intrinsic being, various events, from diverse times and spaces, coincide in their presence with my own subdivided one. I overcame my regression to the year 1953, reincarnating my youth as a twenty-year-old, and now there are other caprices of memory, and they make me set out along the byways traced by my steps when I was a child about ten years old.

I am writing these lines at the same time I am lost in poetic considerations. Suddenly I wonder how to go about describing a wasteland without anything else in sight, something that is more than a sand-filled stretch with nothing but dunes channeled by the sculpting, painting fingers of the wind. Ah, I know now that I am standing in the middle of an absolute desert where, without any prior action, I had already integrated all existing wastelands into the plane of fantasy, even those of the future although they might now be forests or jungles, which in this case already reveal their downfall. The desert has won, banishing all water, vegetation, human beings, and many other living beings from the space its boundaries delimit. By contrast, the imagination of the poet renders it more fertile, living, potent. Nonexistence is a window for the imaginative. I am writing now, describing myself contemplating the desert at the same time. I am thinking that I am thinking, from the vantage point of my modality as an imaginary being, that the vast extension replete with sand is nothing other than a becalmed sea, bewitched by the magic of a poet of infinite powers. I cry out to the poet I am: Create! Now I am in charge, the ethereal one who has been transferred from my mortal being to this naked vastness. I extend my imperious right hand a miracle! the dunes turn to liquid. Now they're waves, they rise up in sinuous walls as high as my will could wish. I have just given life to the ocean. Look! what a nice, lovely, exclusive sea. It's red in color, with countless hues both too many to count and too far beyond the routine concreteness of the material. Let the waters be green! The jungle and the sea run together and merge, and now they rise up, back and forth frenetically: they are making love. Now an ocean of colors inundates the waters, and everything is an iridescent jubilation. I am entertained by the sounds that the oceanic depths emit and the ones that the explosions of the chromous waters produce, against the backdrop of the blue of space. This symphony is also real, like the one held by shells that have been the homes of snails. Fishes of the most varied shapes and colors turn into carefree birds. I am visited by images impelled by other ideas, which constrain my sea to the point of drying it up. I, an imaginary being, am absorbed by the inescapable fact that I am made of clay and that the sea in which I have recently lost myself will waste me away. Whew! I float to the surface and without realizing it I see the lifeless sands, and now all of a sudden, I do not know if what I see is in fact a real sea on which my mind of a haughty poet has imposed calm and silence without any possibility of turning back.

El Huilo, Arnulfo, and this dreamer who is used to traveling via his memories over the permanence of time make up a trio of snotnosed brats so badly behaved and unbearably naughty that nothing like us had ever been seen before. We were between eight and nine years old and we knew all there was to know. As far as being daring and adventurous, as far as I know there was no one who could get a drop on us. Raised in the country setting of a small communal farm, one that was very poor and isolated, we struggled hard to overcome the monotonous drag of a single day, repeated every twenty-four hours, with the intense emotions that come from daring adventures. We went about our business in the context of hills that were always barren, covered on one side by stones and on the other by the dry bed of the Magdalena River, which was something like a millenarian scar, in addition to the intermediary fields of thirsty rows of corn, fields inhabited on the edges by bony-shadowed mesquites, carpets of cactuses armed with threatening rancors. All this was in contrast to the trees and bushes made more animate by the intense green that ran alongside the watering ditches whose water was intended for the nevertheless squalid fruit-bearing fields while at the same time the sucking motion of avid roots reduced their level. We are now beings who are light of foot, sharp of mind, and of a sharp disposition.

Once, in the middle of December, when nights in the desert freeze your very breath, we were playing statues with some other dusty, dirty kids. The usual shouts would reach out to us down the slope of darkness come on in now, it's gotten real dark! you can't see a thing! the Headless Horseman's going to get you! Before breaking up, El Huilo, who by the way is the guide and commander, proposes that tomorrow good and early, you little fuckers, before the sun even comes out, I'll be waiting for you here in the ditch. We'll taking a dive in the icy waters, nude, and anybody who tries to get out of it is a dog's shitty ass and a motherfucker. Ah no, the water's full of ice at that time of the morning. Well, if you don't want to, you're a bunch of dick-faced faggots and, what the hell, you can go fuck your mothers. As soon as it is dawn, Doña Celestial looks at her face in the moon-shaped sea mirror of stars. She has yet to give birth to the Child Sun. Three silhouettes are making their way through the dark. They strip. Their naked bodies stand out. Come on, you creeps! You're next! All the ducks in the water! Hey, you little shit! Come on! Damn, it's cold! Their teeth are chattering and the skin of their hands and feet has turned blue. They run off as fast as they can, dying from laughter. In those days those kids hadn't the foggiest idea of what was meant by moral values. They spied on the stallions and the mares just to see them make a pyramid, joined together in the game where the mast of the animal plunges half-way into the mare, only to withdraw and then to move back in with glee in an energetic in-and-out motion that left them feverish from just watching, as much lost in thought as with their eyes all glazed over. The three Peeping Toms are joined by a pack of snotnosed brats. The favored actors of such a spectacle are a cute little mare and a very tall sorrel stallion. First they whinny, then they paw the ground and nip at each other. They toss their heads and whirl in half circles that send us running to get out of the way, only to return in order to find the best angle so as not to lose a single detail of the crowning moment. Suddenly, the young lady becomes real coquettish and raises her tail slightly to the side, while the acrobat rears up on two legs and places his front paws on the haunches of the lady. Now he's in a vertical position and executes horizontally the penetration with mysterious exactitude, hopping about a bit to ensure the fit. He proceeds to introduce his enormous screwdriver, and she arches her back, and then there they are rocking back and forth, oh my God! The sorrel climaxes and rests his head on the flank of his lover, his neck collapsed. He rolls his eyes back so only the whites show. We all break out into applause, excited by a rare enthusiasm, part human and part something intriguing. . . . All of us kids from the communal farms had witnessed at a very tender age the birthing by females of all sorts of animals. Of course, our intuition led us close to understanding how the rational animal is conceived and given birth to. We also didn't fail to witness the action by which dogs, pigs, and what have you got pregnant. Aside from cuckold angels and a passel of experiences of all sizes and shapes that had invaded out minds, we felt ourselves ticklishly influenced such that a burning afternoon in July we conducted ourselves with Quechita in the grossest manner. For years everyone commented on the dreadful behavior of these three unfortunate lepers. As always, idea became expression in the snout, if not the mouth, of worm-infested Huilito. Hey, do you guys know that Quecha is washing clothes down there in the gully among the weeping willows. She's down their with her grandma, Doña Renga, who's as old as the moon, so much so she's deaf and can barely walk. We're going to get to the girl. Just so you know, anyone who doesn't take her is a motherfucker. Ah, no, ah, no, not that, my father'll beat me to death, shut your trap. I'm out of here too, this business is too much for me, my pa'll grab me by the hair on my head, let's get going, cause he'll like to kill me with a special two-by-four's got my name on it. Well if you rats freak out I hope your mother's tits and her cunt all dry up. Hey, how disgusting, you're going to fuck your own mothers, you faggots, you faggot fairies. La Quecha sees them coming. She smiles at them innocently. Quecha, come on, give me your a . . . What? What are you saying to me, you fucking shitface. Give me your ass. We want ass. Mommy! Mommmmy! Hold on a minute, here I am, what's the matter. Did something bite you? Mommy Renga, those kids running off wanted my ass. Damn you brats! Stop your running. Go fuck your mother, you little turds! Wait'll I get a hold of you, just you wait. History is not only written with letters, but also with the artifacts of war, and on occasions with slaps and blows from a belt.

Here I am again in my windowless office. The year is 1993 and its in its infancy, sending me off to the classroom. I've just finished my sabbatical year, which provided me with the luxury of getting sick. I wrote another novel: *Dead Men Count*, along with a collection of short stories, *Río Santacruz*, and a dramatic work is ready, *Huachusey*. Stories have appeared here and there in anthologies and literary supplements. An Argentine book, *Latinos*, included fourteen of us Latin American authors, and I was the representative from this side. My imagination takes flight in this small cloister, and in turn I dream, sleep, smile, talk to myself, deal with a student, all the while working out a dialogue, a short story or a potential novel. The telephone rings, hello yes. I remain attentive to the visitor while sailing away on a fictitious craft, discovering themes, drawing characters, and everything at the same time. Young Fidencio appears. He reads an allegorical story to me, one whose central character is a small ant. In fifteen minutes I will face twenty-some students on the first day of classes in this semester beginning today.

Someone knocks on the door. It's Walterio, who has the office next door. He's a specialist in medieval literature, a real professor. He pays me a visit to persuade me to send something in to a literary contest in a place called Gardeners. Even though he's a Gringo, he speaks Spanish like an old Christian. You've got to have faith in this contest, man, "The Bronze Syllabary." Just you wait and see, you'll get good news. Bah, literary contests are all laughable. People who win them only prove my point. I could swear to you, Walterio, that Miguel de Cervantes y Saavedra would never have won a single literary prize, so why me. Suddenly, without losing the thread of the conversation, my memory brings back to me the scene of a moment ago when I ran into Dr. Tatum, my friend and chair of the department, in the hall, and he tells me that Camilo José Cela will be awarded a doctorate honoris causa in literature by the University of Arizona. We think it will be in May 1993, so there you are. Well, Maestro Walterio, tell me out of curiosity who the judges are in this contest called The Bronze Syllabary. Well, man, only the most well known names among writers in the Spanish language. Wow, they are sure generous with their time, reading manuscripts by a lot of other people while their own work gets put on hold. No, no, look, people who read a lot of pages are the ones who make up the subcommittees. That way, they filter out all the works that seem to them to be worthless and leave for final consideration about seven manuscripts from which the bigwigs determine the real winner. Well, that's how they do it, my good friend Jorge Manrique, with the result that the bald man will find a curling iron. If the ones doing the initial selection are pedants without much of a standard, well, the end result'll be as expected. Or if they know what they're doing but have specific prejudices and regional preferences, then you can imagine how they'll toss the best stuff in the waste basket and end up passing the chaff along. What's more, Walterio, the one who ends up being the biggest voice among the jurors is the most persistent one with the biggest ax to grind. No, man, listen to me, send something in and hope for the best. We take a liking to Don Camilo. We picked him up on the evening of 12 February 1987. The old fellow showed up accompanied by a thirty-year-old blonde, very solicitous and attentive, always ready to help Don Camilo. Marina Castaño was the writer's secretary, and she turned out to be real talkative with us. She told us about all they had to do in Miami and the comings and goings we could see reflected in the face of the future Nobel Prize winner. The man is picturesque in addition to being wise. His hard face hides a child, one who rather than having been spoiled in his infancy had been hurt somewhat, who knows by what family circumstance, according to the insinuations of my intuition. Of course his writing is good. He provides the shocking character of his writing with an especially personal patina, the consequence of unusual expressions and turns of phrases. Aside from jolting opinions and judgments that are the consequence of aggressive and unheard of contexts bounded by the limits of narrative fiction, his colorful revelations provide unambiguous depictions of tragic and humorous events, all conveyed in an agile and attractive prose, and yet his pages have a certain ironic twist about them, while others are masked by a biting satire. Undoubtedly, wisdom and knowledge inhabit this old man who remains grounded in his youth, in the spirit, much to his good fortune. While I weighed motifs having to do with the visit with which Camilo José Cela honored me, the professor, a mirror of archaic texts, continued to speak to me about that aforementioned literary contest The Bronze Syllabary. Well, yes, but tell me, let's see, why do you think you have no chance to be a winner in the genre you participate in. It's a self-defensive attitude, Maestro Walterio, because deep down I know that whatever I submit will be outshone by something better, so why should I want to pay any attention to that droning on and one where the doling out of literary prizes takes place among a bunch of guys who share the same philosophy and who go out of their way to exclude the Chicano on purpose. Our literature is art, testimony, a flag of rebellion, if you want. We provide a reflection of what is ours, including our popular speech: jargon, slang, whatever expression may be valid for showing our inner feelings. No two ways about it, there are intergalactic spaces between one set of criteria and another. As far as quality and what is authentic, let's leave that to Mr. Chronos. No man, no, there is no place to think about that, where's all this harmful gossiping coming from, I'd like to know. Well, perhaps you're right, Walterio, and this head of mine is slipping and sliding all over the place through an association of ideas. What do you mean? What ideas. The fact is that in Mexico people respect and admire Fidel Castro. Again Don Camilo comes to mind. He told me in a letter that my novel *El sueño de Santa María de las Piedras* is good. But when he was here in Tucson he didn't mention it once. Naturally, I would never ask him to support my books. He's my guest, and as such, he gets the royal treatment. This aside from the fact that in addition to being Spanish, I'm a Yaqui, full of pride by inheritance, full of hospitality out of inborn nobility. He looks at me. Like every writer he sees things and defines them spontaneously. Yet he won't see inside me. Many Mexicans do not like anyone to read our minds, and much less do we like anyone to see our naked souls. He will go back to his country thinking that he spent time with one more jerk. After all, from one writer to another, everybody is on his own wave length, so what's the big deal, if all pantheons are so democratic. This man has his delightful complexities, after all, his intellectual power and a character that is apparently iron clad, and he's probably been vulnerable to the adulation of people wanting to take advantage of him. But in turn he's probably wounded more than one king or important lackey as part of a game, because there's no doubt about his dignity. His legs were swollen as a consequence of I don't know what problem. We took him to a lot of places, but always making sure that he had to walk as little as possible. In the couple of weeks he was here, he didn't walk more than three hundred yards. No, man, there's nothing political about this competition, and there's nothing opportunistic about its organizer, no, what an idea, and there's nothing penny-pinching about him. The goal is much more elevated, you've got to believe it, man, have faith in your fellow men, and with a little bit of luck you'll win. We'll see, said the blind man. The word Gardeners certainly sounded lovely. Besides, it's about time we had a bath in the bathtub that once belonged to a Poncho de Puma.

I'm standing before the students in my course on creative writing, eighteen students of both sexes. We talk together; they ask questions, and one or another of my concepts leads us to talk about language. Pedro Salinas assures us that anyone whose language is deficient, whether he is an athlete, a champion, is as crippled and handicapped in his intellect as though he were lame or halt, handicapped in both his arms and legs. That academician doesn't mince words. As Azorín says, just a few, clear words to create beauty and spark the feelings. Write as you damn well want to, using whatever terms you want, as long as redundancies don't make you tiresome, according to Unamuno. Take Sábato's hand so he can lead you through his "tunnel," so that you can know what is yours. Horacio Quiroga's face, consumed by ants, rises from the tomb among the verdant shadows of the jungle, and I recite to the students his decalogue of the perfect storyteller. There you are, writing is like building a brick wall. You put the first brick down in the form of an opening literary episode, and the rest is child's play, according to García Márquez. The students have never seen a photograph of the famous Gabo, but I am looking right now at his coconut face. I turn around to laugh out loud. So Don Camilo is coming. Aside from his painful extremities, his bone joints bear an extra weight that would undermine anybody's resistance. I told him about the enormous production of copper in the area around Tucson and about how the bigwigs in the city, beginning with the mayor, order the printing of fancy scrolls for illustrious visitors. The truth is that, here, outside the university setting, no one has the slightest idea of the existence of Don Camilo, and he refused to tell anyone about his presence to avoid being bothered. Nevertheless, he became as happy as a little kid who's just been promised a war tank as a toy at the very mention of the copper scroll. Man, how I would like something like that, a copper scroll bearing best wishes from the mayor of the city of Tucson. Boy, that would sure make me happy. I got one for him. The damn thing was ready at the last minute, thanks to a state legislator, Rudy Bejarano, whom Maestro Cela didn't even meet. I gave it to him at midnight just hours before he boarded the plane to go home. You should've seen Don Camilo José Cela's excitement. He clutched the sought-after prize with laughter and joy. The fact was that I had to run from one important person to another, making explanations and trying to be convincing to people that didn't know me either. I got the idea to take along some of the Maestro's books. Then Rudy showed up, my neighbor as luck would have it. We didn't really understand the glorious significance of that copper sheet with a dedication of the mayor to "the great Spanish writer who honors this city with his presence." In the hall I ran into my colleague who's a medievalist. Listen, you left me thinking, tell me, why does Fidel Castro get so much recognition in Mexico. Well, look, I'll pass this along to you. Professor Trigales, from Ciudad Obregón, maintains that Castro taught all the blacks in Cuba to read and then he gave them equal-opportunity employment. He closed the brothels that had been the playgrounds of the Gringos looking for mulatto women. He evened out the economy in order to convert a fratricidal system into a fraternal one. His utopic odyssey against social injustice has blinded him to any strategy grounded in the possible. His passion for the hungry infects anyone who dreams the illusion of an earthly order that is truly egalitarian. His is a hard spiritual struggle against the fragile, because it is most humane, the condition of any people, a struggle that is sensitive to physical suffering and to the abandonment and persecution of his fellow men. So, Walterio, in the end I will send something to that prize competition. Joking aside, the intention of those people is praiseworthy. They are fighting to put our Spanish language in orbit so that it will have a place of dignity in these climes and continue to nurture us with the energy and pride that it bears. Neither bullets nor knives can harm the word.

Well, well, but look, I just found out on the news on TV that Salinas de Gortari scolded Castro for his errors and abuse. I'll bet you don't know that he recently killed his best friend, the general who was in charge of Cuban troops in Africa. Yes, it's true and also very sad. In addition to being a man, man is usually also a jackass. It isn't fair, because jackasses usually aren't men. Frustration is the mother of tragedy. The Castros make mistakes and the whole world makes accusations against them, because that's what the propaganda machine orders them to do. If the powerful countries that absorb the good or bad economies of the weak states engage in genocide in order to steal gold, petroleum, territory or whatever from them because they refuse to bow before them, the publicity apparatus then shows up, transforms the lies that it then institutionalizes, and then we have victims who are villains and the victimizers are shown as heroic guardians of liberty and democracy. Well, well, you'll see how you'll win or at least you'll come very close. Don't worry about Don Fidel because in reality, the only one who'll overthrow him'll be Mr. Chronos, because he's an old man now. The seed is in turn the regression to childhood and the continuity of one cycle after the other, so that when one man dies, from old age or whatever, another one has been born. This takes place in our dimension of temporality. I walk into my office, stretch out on my chair and half-close my eyes. I can't keep from laughing. We received a letter from Don Camilo, filled with newspaper clippings. What? We were flabbergasted. Not only is that man a great writer, but he is the cleverest of mortals. Look at this photograph and the words written at the bottom. Don Camilo appears in the photo with his legs wrapped in gauze or some kind of adhesive tape, something like the kind used for Egyptian mummies. There's a brief accompanying article, "The tireless pilgrim, the explorer of new spaces, the eternal vagabond, etc., etc., etc., Don Camilo José Cela, returns to Spain after a long trek by foot consisting of dozens of miles in the southwestern desert of the United States." There he is smiling in the next photograph. With its accompanying legend. "The mayor of the city of Tucson in the state of Arizona, USA, in an august ceremony extends to the famous Spanish writer Camilo José Cela the keys to the city and a beautiful copper scroll engraved with words of praise." Don Camilo gets the best mileage out of everything, no matter what. Nevertheless, his genius and his humanity remain intact. The man is worth his weight in gold, make no mistake about it. It won't be long before he's here with his wife, Marina Castaño, at his side. The press, radio, television, the telephone, opinions coming and going and who knows what else, they carry our own criterion as a prostitute's pair of undies first showing it off and then covering it up. I yawn and stretch myself out fully. I'd rather not talk about the several hours I spent exchanging cuss words with Don Camilo. Well, all right, but only two or three details. You see, I like to delve into popular humor. I'd like to take stock of how ingenious you are here along the Arizona-Sonora border. For example, we define the concept asshole as the place where the nobility of the spine ends. What would you say, man. Well, Don Camilo, here on the frontier, with Hispanics on both sides, we say that the asshole is where the hide swirls. Hey, that's really great, just great. Do you have a definition for farting? Yes, several, like that theory that says that the fart is a virile protest of one that's stuck sideways. Well, that's certainly an usual one. Let me make sure I make a note of it in my notebook. Now tell me another joke, any one that comes immediately to mind. OK, then, do you know what the vagina said to the heart? No, tell me, what did it say? Let's you and me throb together. Man, congratulations, you people here on the border are doing great. We spent a couple of hours exchanging stupid remarks and the old fellow couldn't keep up with his notebook and pencil.

Sometimes, since I've been a university professor for twenty-three years, and before that I did construction work for twenty-four, including some time in the fields, not to mention my first fourteen years spent on the communal farm in El Claro, where I was raised, precisely, with the impression moreover of everything my father told me about life in the mines where he worked up to the age of thirty, so many situations, images, anecdotes, people from all social levels that I have come into contact with and lived with all jumbled together in my mind, and it's not unusual for me to experience on occasion confusion over a mason, a professor, or a peasant, according to the circumstances. All of these immediately interfacing microcosms are joined by the countless fictional motifs that have acquired existence in the pages of my published books. Because once given literary form there are many characters that assume an autonomy without caring one whit about how surprised the unfortunate mortals are that engendered them. Eventually, individuals who have been invented are no different from those who are from mothers born.

We lived on a small parcel of land among another one hundred and ten that make up the communal farm of El Claro. We took turns at irrigating. The water came from a long slit that ran alongside the river with its sandy bottom and shallow level. Each farmer was entitled to seven acres. Despite the smallness of the plot, my father planted cotton, wheat, corn, according to the season. The uneven struggle was against the bearded darnel that threatened the plants and the bad seed we got from the communal bank, not to mention the many scoundrels who paid a pittance for the harvest long before it was taken in, as a lesson to and vile exploitation of the defenseless laborers. My father lived enslaved to unending labor with no letup or anything else. My poor mother spent the greater part of her twenty-four hours, one shift after another, performing miracles in order to cook us something to eat and wash our clothes, occupied in endless exhausting chores. All this was complemented by the asphyxiating anguish of never knowing where I was, an unrepentant vagrant and still not even ten years old. Her begging, scolding, words of advice, spankings, threats to tie me up, absolutely nothing worked to keep me within the family circle. Since the fields under cultivation consist of a swatch of about six miles in length by about a mile and a half wide, in addition to several thousands acres of dry lands that belonged to the communal farm, the houses of the small town stretch out along the collections of parcels. The heart of the communal farm was located more or less in the middle, nothing but a handful of narrow streets. The western edge of El Claro consisted of the broad bed, full of white sand, of the Magdalena River, with high hills lying in the distance, ridges and short esplanades covered with cactuses and other stubby bushes.

Along the east side, right next to the edge of the town, there is a wall of high hills covered with patchy vegetation. One of the hills consists of a gigantic pile made up of enormous loose rocks. Overwhelming like a wall, this range is an easy climb for adults, but quite a conquest for children. Mystery lies there. It was an immense space that my enormous curiosity as a child adopted as its own territory. Everyday I would explore some stretch of it in every direction. My mother would be sick with apprehension that I would fall victim to its potential dangers, some animal or poisonous insect, sunstroke, a fall, or that I would get off track and not be able to find my bearings, and terrified, she would start yelling for me. On many occasions I wouldn't hear her shouting because I would have wandered a long way off. I've always had a good relationship with the flora and I've always considered the solemn and elegant saguaros to be like my brothers, my neighbors, and guardians because of their height and the multiplicity of images they suggest. Aside from coyotes, hares, a stray puma, rabid dogs, and other minor animals usually found in the desert, in these parts a substantial population of rattlers and other snakes abounds. It is easy to come upon a gila monster. The land turtles are scarce because they are edible. I never knew of any adults who might have constituted a threat. But I do still harbor in my heart the warmth and tenderness so many families in El Claro offered me. My record as a wandering and adventuresome child, despite my tender years, won a lot of kindness for me and a measure of admiration because of my daring and all the tricks I pulled or was caught up in. I was frequently involved in fights with the kids of my age and ones a little bit older. On more than one occasion, when it was getting dark and no one knew where I was, my papa would go out looking for me on horseback. Sometimes the neighbors would help him by fanning out in various directions. My mother, her face a fright, would run about filled with anguish, praying to the saints, the Virgin, God himself for nothing to happen to me. How intelligent was my father's approach. He would pretend to get mad every time I did something really naughty. In the end, he always behaved with so much patience and understanding toward my particular case. How many times I used to return home when it was already night, my feet a mess because of the long and hard spines that would still be stuck in my heels and the bottoms of my feet. I don't know by virtue of what burning fevers and a violent stabbing sensation I barely managed miraculously to save myself from tetanus or gangrene. When my wanderings took me into foreign territories, I and other kids would end up fighting worse than any dogs. These wars would be continued at school during recreation period. Aside from being punched in the nose and kicked, I also came to know about rock-throwing battles. Nevertheless, I would miraculously appear at the end of each day. Calm would return. Night and sleep would drift over us. I enjoyed thinking about the dawn, in order to undertake once again the quest for something indefinable in the reaches that in my fantasy-filled mind would take on the appearance of what was most exotic and extraordinary, never before witnessed by human experience. On one occasion even my father shed tears at the side of my sobbing mother. They were surrounded by sympathetic neighbors who were attempting to console them. That whole day and night went by without a sign of Miguelito. The worst descended on the minds of everyone sitting up because of my absence, despite the many optimistic conjectures. My father had bought me a straw hat, and the wind blew my new hat right into a well. In the attempt to salvage it, both of us fell down into the opening, which was about twelve feet deep. My bones, which were still flexible, survived the blow with little damage. I think I was even glad to be there because I didn't call out for help. When finally they discovered me the next day in the sunlight, I was sleeping peacefully, holding on tight to my hat with my left hand. Everybody was happy and laughing over the return of the prodigal son, and a lot of people hugged me. My mama, weepy and smiling at the same time, put together a banquet with the help of her neighbors. Something else stupid I did because of my energy and my curiosity was when I burned three fully-grown grapevines, filled with grapes and leaves, right there in the patio of the Córdobas. It turns out that the aforementioned grapevines were covered with a branch that people in Sonora called "old man's beard." This is a branch that gets full of little balls or small blooms that end up bursting with a kind of fluffy cotton. Once they are dry these little white dots, under the combined effect of the heat and the wind, expand voluminously and give the appearance of a single uniform mass. It was curious to see how those fine threads covered the grapevines, no matter how high and wide. The three grapevines gave the impression of wearing a very fine and elegant white overcoat. When the atmosphere or fire, which are one and the same in the summer months, dry the "old man's beard" bush, it becomes extremely combustible, more than gasoline, according to what I heard tell, before it would be carried off by a gust of wind or one of the many wind storms, which would look like a snow storm in reverse, going from the ground up toward the sky. When I went up to it with a burning match, that damned "old beard" exploded. Not only did the grapevines burn, but also some of my hair, my eyebrows, and my hands, and the rest of me was so singed that I looked more African than Indian. The next day, Don Estor Córdoba paid an unexpected visit. He apologized timidly for bringing a complaint against Miguelito. The two peasant friends drank and smoked together. Don Córdoba left, not without apologizing a second time. Then my father called me. He did not strike me physically or abuse me verbally. I knew how angry he was because of the disconsolate sadness in his eyes. The look in his eyes hurt me more than if he'd taken the belt to me. This noble behavior of his began to tame my impetuousness once and for all. Despite my devilish ways, I was never cruel with the animals. I inherited from my mother a world of compassion and sensitivity for all defenseless creatures, including the plants themselves and other vegetal beings. Although, certainly, I ended up wounding some cactus or other out of simple ignorance or a sort of expected vanity.

Saguaros and pitahayas and a regional variant called the sinita ended up falling my victims. I would carve the three *M*s of my initials with a knife on their flesh, in the open space between the rows of spines. I would chew daily on a plant that gave off a red sap when you twisted its arms, because I could feel my teeth getting solid. Ever since I had heard it had the property of saving teeth I turned it into chewing gum. Maybe that's why my teeth are still strong and I still have all of them. The original name of the plant is "Dragon's Blood." Here in this region it is known as "bloody." I came across snakes innumerable times. No matter how terrified I was, I studied their rattles and their fangs up close. When they attack, they jump back rapidly. If they find they have an unsuspecting shin nearby, they take advantage of the surprise factor to sink their teeth in and administer an overdose of gangrene in the blood stream. I came to play with a snake who had taken refuge among the branches of a small bush. I thrust a stick toward his small tongue divided into a delta, and the snake produced a buzzing sound almost like a whistling, while at the same time lashing half its rope-shaped body out in an attempt to bite me. I would jump back slightly, only to counterattack, and the snake would once again coil itself, half hiding among the thin foliage. It would extend itself like a spring and then coil back, crazed with anger. I would pursue the mortal game, frightened to death, but with the emotion and agility of a cat. I believe I was trying in vain to cure myself of fear. Nevertheless, my daring never went as far as what my cousin Mario did. He treated us on more than one occasion to a spectacle that not even the most arrogant, valiant and experienced of circus tamers had ever undertaken. His wild animals consisted in this case of mature rattlesnakes. Mario, a string bean of a boy, would manage to grab the snakes by the tip of their tail, next to the rattlers. He worked with great agility, and he'd twirl them over his head like play whizzers. Then he would quickly snap them like you do with a whip. Incredible! We would all be amazed to see how the head of the rattler would snap off. Mario stuttered and he would issue us a challenge: lets ts ts see if you sons s s sof bitchesches can do do do that. I can still see him sticking his left hand in the snake's face, which would lunge forward to bite it, while he would reach his right hand under in a lightning gesture and grasp the snake firmly by the tail. The result: a decapitated snake. Every time we came across a snake, we would all shout together: Mario! Mario! there's a snake over here. Mario would come running, his eyes glowing with intense emotion. Before we would know it, he'd performed his number with masterful efficacy. He never got bitten by a single snake from among the many that he blindly left headless. Something changed in the perception of snakes as soon as Mario appeared, because they would try to in vain to slither away. I don't think even the fire ants would bite him. Because he also liked to sit on top of the ant hills in order to engage himself completely in the task of yanking the hind ends off of the laborious insects. We would go in groups of three and four to find wasp nests in order to stone them. The same would go for jicotera wasps in hollows along the surface of the ground. Our idea would be for them to attack our eyes, as is their custom, and we would defend ourselves with rosemary branches. After these highly exciting undertakings fighting winged beasts, we would frequently return home with our heads and our faces swollen and our eyes almost sunken out of sight with the tremendous swelling. I ended up with my entire body covered with white splotches. My mother ran off to get Doña Chu. The aged miracle worker would smile and give me some sort of concoction to drink as she spoke soothing words to my mother. This brat's not about to die, woman, for heaven's sake, calm down; he's still got a lot of mischief to do, you'll see. Come on, stop crying.

When I was about five years old, I already knew how to read and write. My mother taught me because I would not leave her alone with my constant begging her to read stories to me. She knew English very well. In her rare moments of leisure, she would read books in that language. How I admired her ability to decipher the mysteries of the English language. This all happened to us in a setting absolutely alien to anything that even smacked of literature. The happy fact of being able to read and count on boxes filled with popular books, semiclassics, classics, all by various authors different places and times increased my activity and began gradually to reduce my desire to be outdoors and to sleep like a log. The splitting of my inner being found its origins and resulted in the broadening of the spaces I have lived in and lead me to undertake extensive and frequent expeditions. I am referring to the two cosmos where steps in one and flight in the other are susceptible to bearing us off to unknown spheres, each the setting for potential sensations and discoveries of intense emotions and surprises. One is the interior cosmos that can be contemplated from the mind set free for inventions and fantasies, and the other is the concrete exterior world that is confronted by the vision of our eyes, felt by our touch with our feet firmly planted on the ground. These two dimensions, opposed to each other by apparently unbridgeable spaces, are only brought together and fused in all their being and spirit by the printed word. Only words engraved on the page with ink that oozes from objects that have been handled contain the magic of giving expression to the inner gaze that probes the mind and at the same time the scrutinizing physics of external vistas. Ink acquires life as a consequence of the concentrated attention of every probing reader who is susceptible to moving at the same time in the two cosmoses in question as they are encompassed by a single form, that of literature. Ever since I was a child, my curiosity was won over by all that is encompassed by the phenomenon of language, not as a rigorously formalistic discipline, but as something that occurs spontaneously. Intuition and the pleasurable effort to assimilate turns of phrase and forms that language adopts on the basis of common ingenuity have given me experiences that have been miraculously valid in my attempt to exercise with a sense of humor and joy this predilection of mine for literature, which is something that has paid me back in hour after hour of writing without any regard for whether or not the fruit of my wild vocation will be convincing. The array of languages through which human feelings and activities are expressed is as vast as humanity itself in all its complexity. It, therefore, goes without saying that the only way to understand individuals who belong to multiple sociolinguistic communities, in accord with the level or group they manifest, is by means of the speech with which they are able to communicate. The desire to provide testimonies via stories that are told, written, filmed is the desire to find our own key, grounded in the spirit of what is essentially human. For this reason, I employ the language that is appropriate to what I want to signify, without there being any importance attached to what identifies it and without it mattering what sort of cheerful wink or gesture of displeasure derives from the only judge with the right to express an opinion: the reader who pays to read. The critic has no place of privilege: he's paid for his work. Nevertheless and paradoxically, his work is complementary and vital. So when I was ten I set out to explore hills, high ranges, fields, broad plains, the river, all interspersed with readings that ended up leaving me with the practice and the pleasure of books. My exaggerated devotion to exploring settings distant from my home decreased thanks to new companions in my wanderings who ended up with me in the most incredible situations: characters from Verne, Salgari, Dumas, Dante, Du Terrail's Rocambole, Pérez Escrich, along with so many other authors and their characters drawn from boxes overflowing with books that had come to El Claro when my parents were repatriated from Arizona. Later, when I had turned fourteen, I was the one to emigrate to Gringoland where I had been born and spent a couple of months. I arrived in the company of an uncle, whom I deserted after a week. My entry into the Great University: life, began early, abetted by a certain wealth of preliminary "studies." After spending eight months as a salaried worker with an income that I divided between sending money home to my family in Sonora and paying for my immediate expenses, I felt myself to be in possession of my full manhood and deserving of everything toward which man aspires and desires in accordance with everything that the concept might cover. On the eve of my fifteenth birthday, I decided to reward myself with a gift that matched an urgent need: a lover. In order to talk about this, since it was my first experience, several pages later on I will have to devote several paragraphs to it colored by that romanticism that casts a halo around my first steps as a fiery boy. How many laughable things in contrast to just as many other sad ones subsist in my memory with complete clarity. Nevertheless, not every event is safe from the pruning effect of time when it's no longer a question of how many have gone by but how many are left. Of those remote days of my childhood I also still have dismembered images, simple outlines, as nothing more than places and faces that come to me as from remote distances, something like tints of an indefinable colored print that suggests dimensions, reliefs, silhouettes in accord with the spirit of the topographies made up of strange panoramas, people's faces, chickens, dogs, half-diluted on my smoggy retinas. I tenaciously restore all of the things that existed at that time, of which the passage of time has barely left any trace in my eye's retina. That daily friction of the earth against the atmosphere in its foolish turning and turning erodes and undermines persons and things. It constantly upsets inhabited spaces. I once again set traps for my memories to see if I can catch "something" that I will leave cloistered in these printed squiggles to which my fountain pen is now giving birth.

In order to provide a characterization of strange individuals, those who are one of a kind because they are so original and crazy in their behavior, I would need to arm myself with bushels and bushels of words. It would be worth the trouble to give an account of two or three matters, in the spirit of brevity, concerning certain human attitudes that, because they are so incredible, seem to be invented rather than frightening, something drawn strictly from daily reality.

The annals of history and legend would come up short if the shocking episode in which Plutarco and David fight to the death were absent, with their eyes blinded by blood and their nostrils and mouths bubbling with froth, such that in all the world one and only one of the brave and unvanquished men would remain alive. Each one believed himself to be the incarnation of the sum of power and might, and in order to prove it they had to engage in such a singular and terrifying duel.

The witnesses of this event included Vicenta, a woman of noteworthy features: honorable, of mature bearing, a faithful friend of Christian charity. Another and none other was a footloose boy barely eight years old, barefoot, wearing a pair of worn and dusty overalls with no shirt, black with dirt, his head shaved, except for a cowlick in front like a pheasant.

Bear in mind the fact that what transpired in this strange event has no equivalents among Homeric, biblical, or chivalrous characters of any stripe whatever.

His name was David like the prophet and he thought he was the cock of the walk. His life centered on two objectives: to drink and box it out with whoever would come along. The unfortunate who crossed his path, on any pretext whatever, found himself turned into his opponent. His conversation turned exclusively on the fights he had and his enormous prowess and courage: "There were three little shits and I pounded the hell of out them." "The moment I entered the cantina, everybody shut his trap. Those fags knew what was good for them." "I'm spoiling for a fight and you can bet your bottom dollar I'll show them where to get off." "I have one in mind and I'm going to get his ass going, you don't think so, well, you'll see" "I shit and piss on all monuments, and anywhere they look for me I'll jump right into it right there." "Stand aside, because Big Gimp David's here and I really like bottled pig's piss!"

David had developed an extremely powerful set of muscles, more than normal, from his waist up. His arms and left leg were iron clad as well as flexible, but his other leg hung in the air like a root the size of a thumb and twisted like a braided bracelet, with a tiny foot at the tip of it. His right pant's left covered his shame. People didn't know him by the name of David, but rather Big Gimp. A crutch took the place of his right leg, and it had an iron tip that served less to prevent wear than to function as a weapon. That misbegotten Big Gimp, sneaky and nasty in a way like no other man of mother born, trained daily in the use of such a unique crutch, which he called his "macho" or his "piece of furniture." In the manner of a consummate juggler, he would toss his "piece of furniture" up in the air and catch it, twirling it like a propeller. There was nothing surprising about the fact that his age and the number of years devoted to taming his "macho" were the same. It was more useful to him than any other part of his body. Aside from the juggling exercises, he could out of pure intuition teach fencing on the basis of manipulating "machos." When he brandished it like a sword he was so skillful and precise that it didn't matter if he set out to stab an eye, a belly button, or whatever, according to his will. Moreover, once he put it into action, he used it as a club in the style of primitive man, and there was not a doubt about his delivering windmill-like blows to his opponents in exchange for generously receiving their blows directed at him. A circus performer could not have outdone him in the execution of pirouettes. He'd pull himself together and then twirl like a teetotum on his left foot. His right foot, like a worn-out spring, would slice the air as it dangled. Another one of Big Gimp's notable abilities consisted of his skill at riding any animal you could name with absolute control. He owned a dapple gray horse of a very common breed but one that punishment had made mean and cut down to the dimensions of its owner. David was a Yaqui Indian, with all the good and bad attributes he'd inherited from his great-grandparents. He was constrained spiritually by the rancor of knowing he'd been born crippled and marked for scorn out of tradition by the descendants of the slave-minded white men who'd come from across the sea. His sense of humor was terrible, just like he was. He never had a girlfriend. His overweening pride in combination with his hang-ups as someone handicapped alienated him to the extent of destroying any sense of illusion even before he began to grow.

One day, Big Gimp got himself up in a hat with earflaps, a worn-out shirt, his mouth drooling and his pants unzipped. He spent three days and three nights swilling that cheap and deliberately adulterated booze that the locals call "shit." After such a binge, he was ready for the grave. After sleeping it off like a "corpse," he became possessed by a raging anger. His innards burned with the effect of the drunk he'd gone on. Without giving it much thought his left foot and his crutch led him to his nag. He rode forth from his hut made of ocotillo branches and mesquite logs glued together with mud and galloped up to Vicenta's cabin, quite determined to get himself some of the mescal she sold on the sly. In places where there are no cantinas nearby, there is an abundance of "watering holes" that unscrupulously save the hide of down-and-out drunks. Big Gimp dismounted and went up to knock on Vicenta's door. At that moment the dog tied to a mesquite to one side growled at him and showed its teeth in an insulting, despotic manner, only to the greater displeasure of someone spoiling for a fight. He was a huge mastiff aching to use his fangs. Vicenta, who had come to El Claro from her native Jalisco, loved the dog like a companion in arms, and she had given him the name of Plutarch. Plutarch went wild and yapped out three fierce barks to our peg-leg friend. Ah, you bastard, damn animal, that's how things are between us! You fucking Plutarch, you're cussing at me, me, who aside from being a real macho, I'm a dog just like you. Tied to the tree, the dog had a yard of lead in his favor, so he lunged at the cripple with the intention of getting his fill, only to fall back under the pull of the rope. This bit of ill nature on Plutarch's part offended the brawling Yaqui mightily. Damn Plutarch, so that's where we stand. You're asking me to fight to the death, my little Plutarch. Like you want to really kick me in the balls. Your fucking barking is getting to be a pain in the ass. Well, just so you'll know, you son-of-a-bitch dog, not even an elephant can scare me, no matter how drunk, lame, and crippled I might be. I can take on even the fiercest lion king of the jungle, not to mention a damn fucking dog like you, you stinking bag of fleas. Plutarch, I'm just going to let you have your way, so just hold on, because here I come. Vicenta had heard the snarling of the two dogs from the start and was able to guess the challenge between the two of them. Go ahead and kill my dog, Big Gimp you SOB, and I'll fill your rotten belly with expanding bullets from the rifle I've got right here inside, because you're not going to leave me without protection. And now that you mention it, you'll not get a drop from me, no matter how much you're burning. Well, you just keep in mind, you bitch Vicenta, that your fucking animal doesn't even come up to the bunions on my feet. Ah, well, yes, of course, with that crutch of yours and its steel tip you think yourself quite a man. Nobody thinks you're funny, Big Gimp. Try fighting with your bare hands like real men do, if you think you've really got some balls to brag about, and not a fucking withered scrotum like that goddamn worm you've got hanging there instead of a leg. The allusion to his dry leg struck our hero David, alias Big Gimp, so hard that he cast the crutch aside, fixed his gaze on Vicenta, gave her a disrespectful smile and threw himself on the mad dog, as if he were diving into a swimming pool. Rather than ticking by one after the other, the seconds passed as though they were one long one, while the furious battle took place accompanied by the terrible wailing of the old woman, the barking and growling of the dog, and the smothered curses of Big Gimp, who flailed his arms in diligent anguish trying to grab the other animal with his hands of iron. The biped was bleeding from his hands, his shoulders, his face and the quadruped sank his teeth into the man's rear end. The one without teeth had managed to salvage his neck, although not completely. Suddenly, the crippled man begins to utter curses and oaths; the barking of the dog gives way to a muffled rasping that diminishes in volume, until it escapes completely from his open mouth and dies away. So there, Vicenta, you bitch, if you think this is a dead puppet, it's the fucking peg leg I've had ever since I was born, and you'd damn well better take a look at what you can guess you need the most. While the cripple was wiping his eyes with his reddened and slobber-filled handkerchief, the old lady was screaming and shaking the limp dog. Now you're going to pay for this with your life, you goddamn devil of a cripple. By the time Vicenta had reappeared with her rifle and fired it off aimlessly, Big Gimp had recovered his "piece of furniture." He jumped up on his horse and fled at full gallop having forgotten completely about the bottle of "shit" he'd gone to buy to wet his whistle and put out the fire in his belly.

The story of this man more known by his nickname than by his Christian name abounds in situations that are strange because they are so outrageous. In the end he never killed anyone, and his behavior never went beyond street fights of a certain intensity, one or another disaster he occasioned or that landed him in jail, bloody nose and mouth the result of blows, but ones that never involved knives or guns. As for his "piece of furniture," you could call it an authentic member of that malformed cripple. I remember him with complete sympathy. Although I was only eight years old, he treated me like an adult. With evident affection and mischief he would call me "little fucker." He also insisted that "it's time you really tied one on, kid, aren't you a man?" Once he asked me how many times a day I jacked off, "If you mess around too often you're going to grow a big hair on the palm of your hand." He'd talked to me for a long time about his fights and the imaginary women who "put out for him" as though I was more than twenty years old like he was. One day, pretending to be very serious, he announced that when I had hair on my balls, little fucker, you just let me know, because then you and me are going to walk into that cantina and we're going to knock the shit out of every goddamn drunk in there. He studied my reaction which was between incredulity and pleasure and then the bellicose cripple burst out laughing. "Look here, little fellow, we're going to mash them so hard in the snout that our arm'll come out the other side and then we'll just pull it all the way through. Then we'll send them on their way with their faces on the other side of their head so not even their own fucking mothers'll recognize them. What do you think about that?" One day by accident his bad leg stuck out of his pants and it looked like a hanged rat. He quickly cocked his head and shot me a glance. Then he gently grabbed me by the shock of hair my mother would leave hanging over my forehead when she cut my hair close to my skull so I wouldn't get lice. I pretended I didn't know what was going on and he let me go without saying anything. He hated the rest of the kids in my gang, but the two of us got along because I never made fun of him with insulting references to his handicap. Moreover, I was always sticking my nose in things, and my curiosity led me to hang around the cowboys who were tough from their work on the range, which included getting into trouble and rustling cattle. Not far from my house there was a large tree on the edge of a ditch, and those adventurers would show up there in groups, including Big Gimp. Once, Chutabocas, Blabbermouth, who was wild, knock-kneed, and foul-mouthed, gave me twenty cents to go and call Lamberto names like Burras, She Burros, Fucking Billygoat, when he was watering his horse a few feet away in the ditch. Lamberto had just been left by his old woman for another man. Fucking Billygoat! Not being a stupid man, he lit off after Chutabocas. They started in on each other so hard it sounded like kicks from a she burro. Between one blow and another they hollered terrible curses at each other. Buqui Buitimea told me, kid, get the hell out of here, and I set off like the devil was after me. Panchito, my cousin, made David howl because he got him so mad. Gimp was sitting down when he heard these lines: Gimpy the gimp, red shirt, hound's tooth, sideways turd. The cripple set out after him like lightning on his three legs and my cousin barely managed to scramble under the barbed-wire fence. The cripple also burned down a jail, just managing to get away half-burned to death and with a couple of blisters. His list of deeds is endless.

Before I was fifteen years old, I arrived in Tucson from El Claro, the communal farm in Sonora where I grew up. I kept myself informed from afar of the adventures of that roughhouse with the sad countenance. Now in the nineties, there are very few people who remember him, despite his having been such a topic of conversation. If the earth doesn't swallow you up, time will. The cripple never imagined that his presence in the world would be reduced to nothing more than these passing comments by his friend Mayco, which is what they called me as a child as a kind of joke because I had been born in the United States.

As a part of this university setting—books, students, colleagues, classrooms, hallways—I get lost among so many faces. This is something like trying to give shape to one of those hazy dreams that plop us down in the middle of strange situations and that deck us out, through the effect of oneiric magic, with a personality that is not our daily one, but something that one would call alien because it is so fortuitous. I'm walking toward the cafeteria now. Hundreds of students are going in and out of various buildings. The University of Arizona has a population of close to 40,000 students. Their faces turned toward the sky, the campus has a steady color-filled stream of students that look energetic, friendly, sure of step. There are more women than men, and they lend a beautiful and highly ornamental note among the buildings and people, whether they are outside or sitting in a classroom. I continue along firmly planted on the ground, while at the same time I am a passenger in my dream-reality. The professors, university dignitaries, recently enrolled students, doctoral candidates all greet me with extreme courtesy. They refer with respect to the status that identifies me with this prestigious university: How are you, Doctor. Professor Méndez, what a pleasure. Good morning, Maestro. I have acquired the halo of a distinguished writer and prestige as a teacher. Naturally, I find this situation pleasurable. Nevertheless, nothing, no distance can erase the trail of the days that my life is playing out. My periods as a child, a young man, a mature person, an old man continue to work together to enliven the spirit that has always sparked my behavior. There are none of those banishments. The present never overtakes the past because the traces of the latter stretch out toward the future. Eternity resides in the soul, despite the rotations and wearing down of the body. I have in some fashion been able to transpose all the entities of time to a unique dimension. I erase all frontiers between the reality I see and touch and the ideal held by the mind. I seek out the companionship of the mind, and imagination and fantasy are my favorite friends. What I see and what I think usually awake from their suitable planes without my really having to pay them any heed. The time and space of the brain take on a spiritual form thanks to their infinitesimally instantaneous passage through the soul. Good grief! Not even here surrounded by fellow diners chattering away can I free myself from speculative abstractions. I have to savor my coffee and watch and listen to what is going on around me, admiring the women nearby who have been graced with beauty and other details that make them stand out.

I have been a university teacher for twenty-three years by virtue of my own talents, an assiduous incursion in literature, a certain command of the Spanish language and the slang expressions that go along with it, a full capacity to make my way among these activities, given the continued practice and dedication to extracting the essence from books and the spoken word, and also thanks to that other small thing one might call guts. Before entering the realm of academia, I survived in these United States as a migrant worker, at times suspended high up in buildings, engaged in construction tasks, or glued to farm fields and in anything that would put bread in my mouth and gas in my jalopy. These adventuresome and dynamic twenty-four years as a vagabond, plus my first fourteen in Sonora as a peasant, provided me with the diploma than can only be obtained in that great university that is known classically as The Great University of Life.

The first Monday in September 1970 at 7:00 A.M. something so unusual in my life took place that it surprises me tremendously. In the face of this gulf that divides my world in two, I am terrified by the breach that cuts off the first part of my existence and places me standing before another circumstance totally opposed to all my routine before and after. On this September morning the mirror reflects a strange gentleman, dressed in a suit and tie, wearing expensive black shoes that go well with gray, and a white shirt. His teeth show a smile that contrasts with his melancholy look. Loli smears my hair with a liquid that will keep it combed. I burst out laughing, happy and nervous to the verge of tears. This is my first day as a university professor. Chihuahua!, how did this happen? I never attended school in the United States. To be sure, I graduated twenty-seven years ago from a rural grade school, the Thirteenth of July school in El Claro, Sonora, Mexico. I armed myself with six years of study and went forth into the mundane battle to do something worthwhile with my life. Today I begin, with no prior warning, as a professor in the Spanish department of this Arizona university center. Ah, it's certainly funny. My hands are holding onto a bright, new briefcase. I make the pretense of trying to let it go, terrified. My wife laughs, happy. Scarcely three days have elapsed since last Friday when I say so long to August 1970 and my job as a construction worker, as a peon, and as a mason. Yes, last Friday, at 3:30 in the afternoon, the hour we knocked off, I said heartfelt good-byes to my friends, shaking hands with them and hugging some, my companions in such rough, exhausting labors, yet ones that, after all, were fun and in many cases instructive. They looked at me and at each other with uncertainty in their faces. I found out later that not one of them during the following days would have betted against the proposition that I was completely out of my mind. Which is why I was walking laughing towards my poor car, which has been completely vacuumed out so there's not a speck of dust or lime or cement anywhere, nothing from the natural environment because it couldn't be any other way. Well, so what?, since it won't be driven by a mason, but by nothing less than a real university professor. Loli took it to the car wash, and it looked completely different, all washed off, smelling of fresh essence–why, it even looks new. If by chance it ends up next to the other cars that park together at a construction site, they won't recognize it. Now it's shiny clean and smelling of soap. Overnight it's become a luxury car. I don't know whether to swear to keep it even if it is run down and ready to junk. It's the first Monday now of September 1970. Last Friday, one, two, three days in between, I reached home as always, completely covered with dirt and mortar, my face hanging with exhaustion and lined with the minirivers that flowed from my pores and became wellsprings. Loli, with pity in her eyes, solicitously serves me a lemonade with ice. I'm wearing a metal helmet on my head, some snake-stomping boots, and other clothes bearing the heavy marks of my occupation. No doubt about it, every change hurts, no matter how felicitous. Deep down, like the water in a well, nostalgia is mirrored back at me. Melancholy protects me from the sadness that wounds.

Nevertheless, here I am, firmly installed in my office. A desk, a chair, bookcases, a typewriter?, and those pieces of furniture, are they filing cabinets?, that thing I hang my coat from, the swivel chair, with a cushion and everything, is for me, and look!, air conditioning, this is really comfortable, a telephone, too?, why this is all very fancy. Someone's knocking on the door. It's Dr. Contreras, who ceremoniously and graciously leads me to the classroom. Twenty-five students are waiting for you, colleague. Did he call me "colleague"? The majority are women, with about ten men. I began with a famous saying whose ironic intent my students missed: "As we were saying yesterday. . . ." Just think that this was all the result of a book I wrote that caused a stir . . .

I did not think to comment previously on the exceptional event of which I am the principal actor. My sense of humor, at times slightly ironic, makes me laugh openly to myself. With the papers filled out that will allow me to retire now, if I so chose, I like to go on about the very specific case that refers to the fact that I am a full-time tenured professor of Spanish with a salary that, if it does not make me wealthy, at least allows me to subsist with relative solvency. I believe, although I am not completely certain, that I am the only professor who has reached the highest level within the hierarchy of university professors in the United States without having spent even a single day in a classroom in English, including elementary school. I come here armed with only the six years of primary grades in a rural school in Sonora, located in the communal farm of El Claro, alongside sixty classmates. The requirement for teaching in one of these universities is the Ph.D. or at least to be in the final stages of the doctoral dissertation. As a veteran of twenty-three years in the university classroom, I can now handle myself like a shark in the water. As an author, the same thing happens to me in the world of letters with respect to my territory and beyond. I could thumb my nose freely at the whole academic and literary complex if I wanted to. I also have a full knowledge of this other university, its most profound and lamentable aspects, as well as its happy and fortunate ones as concerns experiences I have had and things I have learned. Clearly, I am referring to the "University of Life" of which I also hold a doctorate in blood and fire, mixed in with the pleasure and the emotion of the unforeseen and the intense. Aside from being a comic actor in the worldly farce, I am a happy spectator with a certain taste for banter. I also note when I see myself in action that I have become something of a braggart, a bit of a heavy, as they say in Sonora. But my age entitles me more than a little to toot my own horn and turn sommersaults. Every older person has every right to laugh at half the world, at himself, and at the individuals who get in his way. Why not, especially if they are fools, as Don Camilo, my colleague, says. Among the gratuitous rivals who have crossed my path in the literary and academic stables, there are various types who die, consumed by the flames of envy, very indignantly, with the mercury blowing its top, all because a poor chump who'd been a mason until one Friday showed up next Monday wearing a gown and mortarboard. Besides, it's one thing to be a frog in a small pond and another to be king of the mountain. There's a saying that I like very much to the effect that not even bad rheumatic fever can take the dancing you've done in life away from you.

I was fourteen years old when I suffered my first deception in love. It was something terrible. I was left with my head swimming, reduced to a rubble of bitterness and resentment, fanned by flashes of nostalgia. My lover left me for her husband. She didn't tell me she was married. My hands were left bereft of her tits, widowed of the touch of her waist, her legs. . . . Because of the absence of her mouth, mine hurts and burns. I need her fire to extinguish my own. In the moment in which her man returned from his painful absence, she disappeared from my arms as if her destiny was the earth itself, which had swallowed her up. I went around shadowless down a long row of days that stretched into months and months. At first, I resigned myself, hurting and everything else. My blood, my flesh clamored for her even during the period in which Father

Chronos in his role as a gravedigger dumps shovelfuls of time on our memories that have claws and bite.

Nevertheless, there exists Someone, the Supreme Being, who is as powerful as he is magnanimous, whose virtues are so great that wherever our tears spring forth, he turns them into laughter. He transforms our most painful woes into simple childish occurrences. He provides the feeling and intelligence so that man learns to be happy in his suffering. He has said: He who pretends to enjoy happiness as a fortuitous grace will find himself filled with solitude. Blessed is he who is generous and righteous in his spirit, for he will be filled with peace and wealth.

At the age of fourteen, my elastic humanity with all its springs predisposed for the feline attack or whatever adventure would come along, in addition to my energetic mental predisposition for the unusual, saw me with one foot still in infancy and the other on the border of the already intuitively exciting stage of youth. At that age I was already a young man with absolute freedom to determine my behavior in accord with my desires. My entire family was on the other side of the border in Mexico. One more citizen in my person reincorporated himself in the heterogeneous population of Gringoland, the country where I had been born. There still was a large number of U.S. soldiers stationed overseas in 1944. Thus crossing over the barrier into Arizona with my birth certificate in hand and joining the union of construction workers was the simplest of undertakings. They would not take me on in the factories, which were just starting to spring up in what was still a small city, because I was too young. The construction industry is usually dinosaur-like in its primitiveness. I trained daily in a more than brutal exercise, one that devastated energies that were fortunately replaceable by others of greater resistance. My body and my personality were transformed by circumstances from one day to the next, between laughter and joy that hurt. My physique required quantities of food of every kind and taste. At the same time, my preference for voracious reading and developing ideas, anecdotes, poetry, all simple as a pastime with the idea of developing myself was joined by the new experience of discovering colloquial language in all its multiple contents, intentions, and forms. As the result of such diversions, I grew full of potential as much in the material plane as in the other that resides in the brain itself.

In those days, after hard days in the construction of houses and other buildings and with the earth put to bed in its soft shadows and my skin freed from the blistering sun, I used to entertain myself in the company of a group of kids running around the streets, climbing trees, or sitting around talking. The latter childish outbursts were overshadowed by the explosive emergence of another mysterious and exalted stage. I began to be invaded by an exterior, unknown passivity in contrast to another interior disquietude that was dynamic to an unforeseen degree. At the time I felt impelled by an imperative curiosity to penetrate the field of letters with the spirit of an adventurer, I turned quiet and meditative. Moreover, the influence of a new factor overtook me with obsessive tenacity, one that was very effective in altering the functions of my daily thought as well as those of my organism. I found myself in love with the idea of love, and I couldn't sleep for being pursued by sensual fantasies. On the eve of my fifteenth birthday, my brains and my blood had conspired peremptorily to demand I take a lover, an Eve with whom to fuse myself and break free, at the risk of seeing my inner being burned to a crisp for not achieving it. Perhaps the fact of being by this time an assiduous interloper in books by authors of great prominence, in addition to ones who were modest and secondary, plus the premature situation consisting of earning a salary by working eight hours a day in labors befitting hardened men, encouraged me to undertake other weighty activities. Add to this the unique case as concerned my early, absolute liberty of action, given the fact, I repeat, that since the age of fourteen I had been separated from my family in an almost completely exotic country, despite the fact of its being my native country, because I had no other road to travel except that of adventures that temper and predispose man toward certain "undertakings" and spectacular successes.

So in order to arm myself as a knight, one neither on foot nor on horseback, but rather one who is migratory and travels by bus, I required a certain kind of baptism, the confirmation that would provide my person with the characteristic seal of someone who knows what he is doing and who is up to whatever comes along. In the first place I would have to arrange, by fair means, with mutual consent and with equal attraction, the act in which ecstasies, arousal, fire, and, in synthesis, the highest of pleasures, takes place between a man and a woman: sexual love, with all the energy and the feelings that predispose two beings to come together in a spiral similar to the one that produces the birth of the stars out there in the cosmic spaces where mystery and the universe perpetuate a most sublime omnipotent will.

I did not realize at that time that the turning world might be my personal orbit, for I was superlatively oblivious to it. The only ones able to understand my case in those days in which my spirit clamored for nutrients in enormous quantity of letters were the Díaz Pulido brothers, who were from Spain and the owners of a bookstore where I would go to buy books and magazines, despite the fact that the public libraries and the university provided me with material to attenuate my anguished hunger for enlightenment. I am now able to reconstruct the scenes that occurred weekly, in which a tall, thin, beardless boy, burned by the summer sun, engaged in animated literary conversations with a couple of gentlemen of obviously advanced age, who looked on him with astonishment.

The result of cohabiting with mythical entities in so many novels and as part of a daily routine with so many individuals of flesh and blood was that I was not overwhelmed by the confusion of passing from the solid to the ethereal in two different spaces at the same time. Nevertheless, on more than one occasion as I wandered around my adopted land and its outskirts, still lost in unreal dimensions, I felt myself to be in the fields of Montiel or those of La Mancha, not to mention in a hovel and oppressed by lacerating ramblings like Raskolnikov himself, clutching the left hand of the poet Virgil in the face of vile demons and punished sinners, lost in the labyrinth like Segismundo, or even a pilgrim in the jungle or on the Pampas like Cova or Martín Fierro. The ebullience of all this, along with the explosive awakening of my nature, predisposed me to speak in such a way or with reference to things so much on the margin of the setting in which English, Pachuco speech, weak or garbled Spanish would cover the vast extension of the existing sociolinguistic context. My curiosity and my boundless love for the Spanish language awoke along with me. When in the United States I contrasted the English language in the mouths of overseers and all kinds of persons who were indifferent and ugly toward our extremely humble conditions as migratory Spanish-speaking workers, exiled by poverty and despair, I turned to books not only out of congenital love but also as the best refuge and the friendliest isolation.

All this effervescence of ideas, themes, upsets, in addition to the feelings of my intense awakening, left as a deep impression in my consciousness the belief that the only means of making a way for myself in the face of stumbling blocks and prohibitions would be for me to come to terms with my adolescence without ignoring my youth and to be by the power of a courageous spirit a man consumed by the right that daring and experience confer, which in the process would bring with them vast knowledge. Ah, but in order for this to take shape much beyond a simple chimerical state, it would have to become as real as the feline cries and scratches of coital spasms. So, I threw myself into the street in search of the female. I scouted around fashion stores, lunchrooms during the day, middle-class nightclubs, but not the low-class ones. I explored every public place, searching for a young woman who would show me in one fleeting moment what one can never learn in books, no matter how many he reads.

Far from achieving the success I dreamt of, I came to understand that my timidity in direct communication was aggravated by the inhibition in my behavior. I knew deep down that my goal would be an extremely difficult and risky undertaking, since from the outset it excluded any commerce with prostitutes, and she would necessarily have to be, if not a virgin, at least a woman free of the taint of wickedness. I half accepted my defeat because of my lack of expertise in amorous strategies as an orphan in the realm of precise words and actions at the right moment. I would never reach Rome without help. I turned to Rooster Romero, a fellow worker, famous for his success in the area. When I knocked on the door of his hut, he answered solicitously, with a beer in one hand and a cigarette hanging from his mouth. He listened to what I had to say, smiling with his mouth half open. When he heard with surprise what it was I needed so urgently, he stared hard at me for a few seconds and then burst out laughing with brash frankness. The jerk even grabbed his belly. He sagged against the wall while fire came out of his mouth as though his guts were ablaze. He answered me in his unique way that matched the picturesque speech of common folk along the border, which is basically derived from an ingenious deconstruction of Spanish and English, along with other foreign words, which I choose not to go into at this moment, although I will give an idea of the extremely vulgar manner in which that barbarian gave color to certain ideas from his savage harvest.

Well, yes, no doubt about it you're grown-up little fucker. Now if you've started getting the hots, it's time to get out there and sow your wild oats, and all you've got to do now is to find where to do it, pal. Let's see. No, you're not bad looking, maybe your puss is a bit baby-faced, but that's not really a problem. Although it's true you're too serious. You don't roll when you walk and you don't laugh or gesture or make faces or stare when you talk or walk. Besides, you talk too nice. You know what, kid, move your body and talk like one of the guys, and, bingo, you'll be right on. If you really want to make it with a good piece, get with it, man, get on the bandwagon, or else you'll get left behind in the dust. First of all, go to dances. If you don't dance, you're nowhere as far as getting any action, good, regular, or next to nothing. That's what dancing's for, get it? You can always tell right away if the dame wants to get something on with you. You've got to make eyes at her and show her your teeth. If you look all dreamy, you're just about home free. When you get out there on the dance floor with her and they start up the first strains of the music, take her by the arm, like a real gentleman, bro. Show her you know how to move with grace. Tell the girl she's a good dancer even if she's stepping all over your bunions. The first chance you get, tell her you think she's one smart gal. As soon as you sense there's some kind of, you know, feeling between the two of you, take her hand. Don't squeeze it like it was some kind of goddamn lemon, no sir. Just start caressing the back of her hand like you didn't even know you were doing it and then turn her hand up and start working on the palm. Once you're out there on the dance floor with the other couples, fellow, hug her and hold her, really careful like, as close to her ovaries as you can. Look, right here between her kidneys and her pussy. When you're dancing back and forth, try to place your leg between hers, and if you go too far, just twirl her around a couple of times and she'll forget. If the music's just right, you can move and twist your chest a bit and give her melons a bit of a jiggle. When you're dancing cheek to cheek, talk her up in her ear; find any pretext to get close to her ear and whisper yes, yes, yessss. That way you'll blow in her ear and set her on fire. When you're not dancing and you're with other people, act real cool so she won't think you're a dud. That way she'll think you're discreet and know how to get to the honey without startling the bees. And don't go thinking that you're going to get her just like that, no way. Because no matter how much she wants it, you've got to get her in the palm of your hand. Learn how to get their stars down, which is what the dames around here call their panties, in case you don't know. There's always the chance that when business gets going, all you'll get for your troubles is a couple of slaps on the face and a few nasty words. Well, once things do get rolling, all wetlike, and you're off where there's no one else around and it's dark, that's where you need to be, because that's when she'll really start acting like a female, and the rest depends on your piece. She'll know what she's doing and what you want, but the game's got its rules and either you play by them or you get knocked out of the ring. Don't grab her by the butt like a jerk, go slow like an expert. First, a couple of kisses with love bites, her ears, her eyes, her neck, and then the real stuff on her mouth, with your hands going like they no longer belong to you. Your hands are your partners, pal, wiser and sharper than Solomon himself when it comes to things like this. And love sparks all of it! After two or three attempts to get away, her tits are yours. We're really on our way south now, bro! Your hand is now pure poetry, and your fingers are all poets. Stay back, night! Tell her she's got a piano between her legs, and you're going to play one key after another. Before she can pull your ears off, lift her legs to the sky and, real careful like, take your cock, hard as a cannon, and pass it through her spider's web, so swell, there where her body and soul come together. If she pulls away shrieking, don't offer to take her to a doctor. No, friend, that's the way these gals sound when they get all emotional. After working so hard to get there, don't end up doing what so many jerks do whose nerves can't take it. They get all scared, and instead of a hard rod they end up with a flat balloon. So then, pal, good luck and go dip your stick. You don't want the water to get low. Come talk to me if you need some more advice, don't hesitate one bit, OK, good buddy.

Rooster Romero was leaning back in his rocker, hitting the floor with the palms of his hands and laughing like a fool. I left, furious at myself for being so stupid. Where'd I get the idea to seek advice from a pig like him, a real lout, a true shit. What ever gave me that idea I should tell my most intimate feelings to someone capable of riding roughshod over what someone would tell in confidence with no respect or even the faintest idea of what honor is and the obligations it demands. I can just see myself undertaking the sort of program this animal suggested to me, dancing and climbing all over someone just like some whore in a brothel and legions of men who imitate them in public without a shred of decency. What is worse, these dirty rituals get grown and even old men to lower themselves to acts and behaviors proper to eunuchs. Nice advice from a neighborhood pimp, the sort who's used to feeling butts, ovaries, tits, bellybuttons, just like a doctor who deals with hemorrhoids. And I'm not the sort cut out for spending my time squeezing titties and cunts, as though they were tomatoes in the market. I will not assault women in vacant lots in the middle of the night, because I am a man and not a dog or a poisonous insect. At fourteen, I am a man of ideas and concrete actions, with no time for playing a buffoon or a clown in love battles for which I'm just as capable as anyone. The hammer and anvil of the ages have now tempered the size of things that had given fire, hardness, and torrents to the mast with which progeny is forged in the interior spaces of the female.

A bit more serene after weighing angles and possibilities and feeling somewhat crushed, I deduced that perhaps my goal of knowing carnal love thanks to a clean battle and on equal terms with a young lady with similar expectations, would not be likely before the age of thirty. Concerned and saddened, I remembered what Saint Paul had said, "either you marry or you'll burn," although the fact is that matrimony was not my goal, but rather the knowledge and experience that bring power and consolidate man on the highest plane of his integrity. No, there was no question that I would have to wait years—who knows how many?—until my wedding night, and there was nothing else I could swing right now.

Yet without the will of he who determines everything, not even one leaf of a tree moves. It is he who puts the light in the eyes of boys and girls who fall in love for the first time. When he tells them: Reduce your beings to only one, expand your extremities to eight, and vigorously attack each other trunk to trunk, this is where the miracle takes place. And so what I sought came to pass, by chance but not fortuitously.

I would return from work to my room in the opaqueness of those summer afternoons, bathe hurriedly, put clean clothes on, and go straight to a grass-covered park dotted with enormous ash tress, svelte eucalyptus, mulberries, pines, and other trees with foliage merciful in its freshness and friendliness, not to mention bushes that looked like miniature forests, with a fountain in the middle and a drinking fountain to one side. I would show up with my books to read and observe with a sharp eye the world around me. Every now and then I would lean back and close my eyes to doze or let my mind wander in ways that would turn me into a fictional character among the inhabitants of one of my Platonic worlds or, rather, I felt like a participant in the place and time where my tangible humanity was located, alongside ordinary people of flesh and blood that would not go away, no matter how insignificant they were.

I noticed a couple of lovebirds caressing each other among the late-afternoon park goers. They were attractive and would hold hands and emit resonant silvery laughter. What gave an extraordinary touch to this pastoral scene was the presence of a tall, svelte girl with a very beautiful profile who always accompanied the aforementioned turtledoves. This of course intrigued me, and I instantly wrapped it in fantasy. I transformed what was a perfectly spontaneous and natural presence into an apparition besieged by mystery. For the time being, I had no excuse to approach them no matter how hard I worked on it. I knew from experience that not to use words and gestures appropriate to the setting at hand would invariably provoke misunderstandings on the part of my interlocutors.

Those who have been appointed to comment on the Eternal Book certainly have it right. Someone great who in turn invents us, moving and activating us in undertakings that are as complex as they are diverse, as though writing a multiple and eternal novel that splits into infinite times and spaces, predisposed that she and I, microscopic specks of his universal calligraphy, become united in the space of an infinitesimal fraction of cosmic time and in an equally minimal point on the orb.

Our paths crossed in the park for two or three days without any significant modification. I could no longer read, but only gaze out of the corner of my eye at the tall, pretty young woman who walked with such grace. The key moment, the prelude to others filled with pleasure, occurred when we both headed for the water fountain at the same time. I was able to get a full view of her distinguished bearing and to see how obvious her fine sensuality was. Her eyes, intense with tenderness, smiled at me, accompanied by a barely perceptible gesture of curiosity. I let her go first. I couldn't help but admire her while she was drinking. Her thinness was well proportioned, and her hips and breasts were just the right size. Her legs and neck were long, and her back had a discretely graceful curve to it. She was completely feminine, the instantaneous depository of the ideal love that my illusion had been conceived for an eventual full and energetic birth. She looked at me cautiously and with a somewhat furtive glance. Perhaps the bad effects of hard work, plus the traces on my skin of the onslaught of exposure, made me look like I was seventeen. Only my super-sharp sense of observation could reveal to me in a fleeting glimmer a very slight imbalance in her extremely attractive eyes, due perhaps to their being just a little and almost imperceptibly crossed. She asked me some questions with a captivating curiosity, where I was from, what I did, who I lived with, and so on. I invited her to have a soda. She spoke Spanish mixed with words from English with a Gringo accent. Perhaps she noted in my own voice the effort I was making to be agreeable and attractive toward her. I observed a rare enthusiasm in her laughter. Her conversation was a bit overwhelming, which indicated a latent nervousness. Why? Suddenly in a moment when she let down her guard I saw her face fully. She was missing half of the right side of her lower lip! I was able to perceive a brief shadow in her expression, when she saw something in me, how I don't know. We sat down in the shade of an ash tree to eat an ice cream cone. I told her about my situation and she caught my isolation and many other things that one can communicate through trivial words or with the merest inflection of voice, gestures, and those mysterious depths that float around individuals, which are what allow them to tune into the vibrations others give off. In that fashion, through intuited emotions the feelings that in the end might be significant become established.

She introduced me to her sister and brother-in-law, who appeared to be pleased about our sudden friendship. When I indicated to them that we would take a walk around the park, he said, be careful, Bartola! in a festive tone but with a certain intention that I thought I caught. The June afternoon, dozing under the warbling of singing birds and the cries of noisy children, cast shadows on us such that our happy youth shone with the pleasure of jubilant and excited manifestations of love. We were both hungry for love. We kissed with passion. I observed how she compensated with her tongue for the part of her lip that was missing. Her mouth seemed fleshy to me, a very respectable antechamber of other delights never to be equaled by either nectar or ambrosia.

I didn't sleep that night. I laughed for no apparent reason. I felt her, I sensed her: her restless hands, her shapely waist, the softness of her breasts, her burning, damp mouth. . . . I knew then that illusions glow in the dark just like stars. Things were even better the next afternoon. Her companions decided to go to a neighborhood theater where they were showing the movie *God Will Repay*. The two of us stayed talking for a long time among our friends and accomplices of sap and leafy green. The delightful game began at once. We astutely allied ourselves with the less frequented fronds. The few words we spoke were smothered by a string of kisses. So much love and so many caresses gave wings to time, and we glided swiftly over hours counted by the minutes. Father Sun, despite his being zealous and careful, had already been blinded by night. Our indifference complemented our bare surroundings. Leaning against a eucalyptus, we were carried away by a kiss as though it were a raging stream. I undid the buttons of her blouse to make room for my hands and to give my mouth access to her swollen nipples. I trembled with urgency, fear, happiness, and other unknown effects. Then she grabbed my right hand and placed it at the level of her miniskirt, between her legs disturbed by a series of internal bolts of lightning. Her generous hands gave autonomy to mine and they were my best allies, as they felt up her quivering thighs with the precise touch of a blindman. My two hands came together and installed themselves in her most secret anatomy. The sensitivity of my fingers felt the fine hairs that veiled her pubis. . . . With my pants and other garments having been yielded up, her small hand took the trunk of my rod, and she pulled me toward her as she leaned her back against the grass and gripped my waist with her legs. She pushed against me and I plunged into her. The two of us, dual worlds, moved gently, forcefully, slowly, strongly until an intensely brilliant light fused us in one pleasurable agony from which we emerged exhausted and profoundly happy. For three days we lived an unbridled passion in which blood and spirit are completely fused to produce a single material replete with strange powers.

In my hours of daydreaming I came to think we could never be separated. Of course, matrimony was a must. I deduced from a delirious jungle of ideas that for woman to be perfect she would have to be missing half of her lower lip and to give the gift and privilege of each eye looking off in a different direction. The first would be necessary for her to have a tiny mouth, a pretty tuft of fine silk. And of course mystery, fantasy, or nostalgia emanate from crossed eyes. Just to see them with a look of surprise, each one after the same object via different routes, is moving and inspires affection. All of this is a prior condition to being a sea of tenderness, elastic in very agile movements, appropriate to pleasing whims with complex requirements.

Nature is usually very wise and full of foresight. If certain senses or organs are missing, others sharpen with an extremely intense efficacy. I know what I'm talking about. It is not in vain that the object of my adoration moves her enchantments about in a copulatory trance with so much authority that one could say her hips, breasts, mouth, her whole humanity are inhabited by a goddess that would make Venus herself envious. The inner walls of the seat of her delicacies narrow and expand rhythmically to the point of making the irises of my eyes go blank as a consequence of the ecstasies in which sensual pleasure culminates.

My lover who was heaven sent was the model of modesty. We will learn together, my love, she whispered in my ear. Inspired and valiant, we dedicated ourselves to providing the occasion with the appropriate style that would allow us to adapt ourselves to our environment, toward achieving in this way that our occupation would go unnoticed while not prejudicing our amorous endeavor. She took to wearing a very full dress that could be opened suddenly to provide us refuge as though it were a tent. How many times we were seated facing each other appearing to be shaken by earth tremors. Standing with apparent innocence, our lovemaking looked like the convulsions of St. Vitus' dance. She would try out various poses in the afternoon, the proof of her fine talent and creative gifts. Alongside her energetic condition, her artistic vocation was always completely faithful.

Yet nothing lasts forever. That was said by someone who doesn't have to think because he knows everything. It is enough for him to intuit in order to believe, to contemplate in order to know. All that is vanity perishes. All animate material turns once again to dust. The flesh rots so that worms may eat their fill of it. Love, joy, hatred, sadness, laughter, tears, pleasure, tedium are all vanity. Nothing that is of the earth lasts. Even memory vanishes into thin air in the shadows of death. My Lord, may it be your will that souls transmigrate.

Where is she, I can't find her, she hasn't come, I really need her, what's going on, why has she gone away, she must be sick, did she die? She's leaving me, she's forgotten all about me. I've inexplicably lost her! Nothing, not a trace to help me find her. I ransacked afternoons, I scrutinized dawns, I broke down the hours in vain. I rushed around corners, attempting to make her presence out in the distance, just like a crazed wolf cub, because she too had given me her avid breasts to suck. In the end exhausted, I decided to mount a guard in the park, the nest and collaborator of our lovemaking, the witness to our pledges. In the midst of the ephemeral, the glory of a butterfly survives the passing of love with all its iridescent majesty.

One dying afternoon when there was barely anything left but a glow of light, I made out under the streets lights the duet with which she used to form a trio. I run up and stood in front of them. I didn't have to open my mouth. My eyes inquired first. He's come back from his months-long campaign. Who? Kid Tornado, the boxing champion. Boxing champion? Yes, Bartola's man. They had a child, they're finally going to get married, the child's asked them to, he's so lively, they've been sweethearts since when they were students. But . . . it she . . . , I didn't, she never told me. She's a godsend, even if she's a bit cross-eyed and has a harelip, she certainly isn't a bit bitter about it, quite the contrary, she always does her bit and that's why she's happy. While her man breaks his back to earn his daily bread, she patiently waits for him, providing succor to whoever asks for it. When she saw you looking so like a child and alone, she told us she'd become a child too to bring out the happiness that is so natural at your age. Her son is on vacation in Los Angeles, with his grandmother, he's a year or two younger than you are. We're off now to the Flamingo, that night club that's two blocks from here. Come on with us, if you'd like, and you can meet Kid Tornado, he'll like you, he's very popular and affectionate with youngsters.

I followed them as though in a dream. A seventh sense, with all the potential of my cerebral resources, busied itself in reassembling so many scattered fragments.

We came across them. The woman of passions with the face of a vivacious dove was hanging on the arm of a cheerful man whose jovial face revealed even from a distance the bumps from tremendous pummelings. She greeted me happily in English. *Hi, how are you!* Her sister-in-law made the introductions in English. *You know, Kid Tornado, we met this little boy in the park. He came from Mexico, and he lives alone by himself.* When Kid Tornado heard that they'd met me in the park and that, despite my being an adolescent, I lived alone like a puppy without an owner, he told me kindly and with a touch of pity in his mangled Spanish, You're very strong, if you wanted to, you could become a boxer. Go see a movie, kid, he told me in a friendly manner and put two dollars in my shirt pocket. *Good luck, kid . . .*

With the day dead, I discovered that if it's true that stars and illusions twinkle at night, it is no less true that when a "real" man experiences great suffering, he wants to go to heaven and talk to the stars. The anguish of that man is so strong and his wings are so broken that the stars come down to console him and be one with him in his suffering, and in this manner they emerge radiantly in the cosmos of every tear and roll with them down the very dust of which we humans are made.

Here now in the nineties, half a century after the stars wrapped in tears caressed the face of that adolescent in my first encounters with the cruelties that are a usual part of reality, I turn my eyes toward heaven. Then I sweep them along the surface of the earth from one vista to another, without finding any release from the sadness that shrouds my spirit in darkness because of someone I will never again see on the face of this earth that is us and of which we are made. My brother José, Che, has died. He came down with an incurable disease all of a sudden. Nevertheless, the perverse negligence of a dishonest doctor hastened his departure.

In the midst of so much chaos, disorder, cynicism, indifference, and departures from what constitutes justice in its proper sense, we contemplate with astonishment the arbitrary relativity into which it is diverted and deformed. Justice is used to wearing ornaments of false integrity. She now appears naked, pleased with herself over her true name: Dame Corruption. Everything in the name of money and power, which perverts everything, beginning with people's conscience. Nevertheless, in order to keep faith, let's hold onto the consoling idea that the exception is the rule, faith in him, he who knows how to read the specter of specters, both the signs of acts of dignity and the stigmas by which each one of us is deserving or responsible for the conduct of our life in this beautiful and so maligned world.

The day after burying Che, I took a plane to Lansing, Michigan, invited by the Department of Romance Languages of Michigan State University to participate in a congress of teachers of literature, in celebration of the fifth centenary of Christopher Columbus's feat. I saw for the first time navigable rivers, the Great Lakes, and the forests. So much beauty, vitality, stretches of enormous, shady, thick trees, the infinity of small lakes scattered up and down the vast topographies unfolding before my fleeting celestial vantage point from on high. They made me feel overwhelmed. Witness with joy the work of the hands of God covering the surface of the planet. Witness also the grandeur of the heavens I have always seen in the nocturnal display of the stars, of whose making I am but the atom of an atom.

Once on firm ground, I saw many trees and plants, all very beautiful and with names unknown to me. I reduced them all to pine trees. I participated in the aforementioned symposium with talks for dozens of graduate students. I visited six schools, including elementary and secondary. I spoke to audiences filled with colleagues about literary creation, knowing full well that it is a matter that will never be totally explained. Young blacks predominated among all these students. They understood me and we got along fine, despite the fact that that was the first occasion for me to express myself in English. My colleagues and everybody else treated me like a king, like a saddened king.

Strangely, on my way back to Tucson, I occupied myself during the flight that lasted several hours by writing a couple of pages about rivers without water, the rivers of my childhood. I wrote about the time, which was extraordinary because it was extremely mysterious, in which I had an encounter with "time" in person. . . . Despite the fact that it revealed itself to me so confidentially, I was unable to recognize it at the time nor for several years afterward. It's only been now that I have been able to grasp its meaning, during these last few nights in which, a little bit on the desperate side, I make something out, some sign that would indicate to my intuition, with a brief glimmer, what we are forbidden to know of those great mysteries, we who are only passing through on our way to a certain end.

To contemplate the desert rivers, to walk their dry courses, to weigh in one's hand the stones from their beds, to see, standing in the very center of their bowels, the walls, the banks, the meadows in the distance, to feel myself here, on the inside of the vast channel, produced in me an intense excitement, one that was unexplainable at the time. The course of the Magdalena River, which a few kilometers down takes on the name of the Assumption, is relatively wide where El Claro is. Nevertheless, when I contemplated its center from the perspective of an eight-year-old, its spaces seemed immense to me, and I became excited with the feeling that I was enveloped in the specter of its currents. Both my vision and my sensibility became mysteriously altered and my perceptions and other undeniable senses became confused. The course of this river drew me like a magnet. Despite the fact that it was a long way from my house, I would go to visit it doggedly. The river and its influence hypnotized me, bending me to its bidding and bearing me to its heart to explain intimate things to me about its very remote origins. Whenever it rained like mad, the brooks would flow into the Magdalena, filling it with ephemeral water, a flow desperate to join the Sea of Cortés before it could be swallowed up by the calcinated rocks and the thirsty sands. Night would amplify the roar of the chocolate-colored flood. I would make out its open, subaquatic voices and its various registers, until my eyelids would cover my eyes like the curtain of a theater filled with imagination.

During the day, I found one way or another to escape the watchful eyes of my loved ones. I would go right up to the very edge of the express train to closely examine, unwittingly daring, the yellow water in its headlong rush, shoving before it and bearing, tumbling, and whirlpooling, all kinds of passengers on its crest: uprooted trees, swollen cows. I saw two horses gripped with terror. As they neighed sharply, they thrust their heads and necks forward, nipping each other with the white edge of their piano-like teeth. Household objects and deformed shapes would file by. The immensity of the water would keep on coming in acrobatic waves, threatening the high walls that held its boundaries and devouring them in its hunger. Dumbfounded and thrilled, I would stay for long periods admiring the dynamics nature would show, this time represented by the Magdalena River, until someone with the authority of being older than I was, would order me emphatically to go home immediately.

Now that it has occurred to me to delve into the actions of those days, I find that the uneasiness with which I would lose myself in the middle of the sandy river was in effect a dizzying discord that was due to how, thanks to magic of the setting, I confused space and time.

The spirit of the river had the power to overwhelm my soul of a child and to make my already sharp sense of perception and isolation hypersensitive like those minds that are already predisposed to knowledge, like a new film that engraves and imprints images in their smallest details. The fact that I had the impression of a vast breadth and that the river would grow in an illusory fashion into a giant before my eyes, when in reality it was no more than a bed of ordinary width, owed itself to how in some strange way the atavistic meaning of the river transferred itself to my childish consciousness with all its weight of millions and millions of years together. I sensed in the river the aged presence of a common grandfather, one who was above all things and individuals that could be found in the context of the universe. Nevertheless, I saw his prodigious age and his vast borders translated into simple elongated spaces.

What is broadest in relation to this river is in truth time. The space demarcated from one bank to another, seen in its precise equivalence on the ground, is no more than a stone's throw. It was he that I felt in the blunted stone forms with the seeing touch of my childish hands. I was enchanted and intrigued, without being able to explain it with complete clarity, by the sense of the millions, billions of years imprinted on the soft and rounded texture of the stones, not to mention the flat stones, which looked like coins with rainbow specters minted by him, my supreme grandfather, who availed himself of the magical pottery making that pulses in the diluted hands of the water.

How beautiful rivers are. As a man of the desert, I am captivated by the rivers with their beds of sand and stones, because when I was a child they told me ever so many stories about their long-ago lives that took place throughout the length of rushing waters and waterfalls for years and more years, one not registered by history because Father Chronos had not yet learned how to keep track of those distances in those days and still less to measure their indivisible flow in periods of time and intervals.

Now at this very moment, I am in an airplane on my way back to Tucson. I've been in Hermosillo. I am flying right over the area where I spent my days as a child. In a few minutes I will make out my communal farm, El Claro. Simultaneously and moving backward, I descend through time over the period in which my first years slipped by. I glue my eyes to the window, sharp and wide open. I can see the barren plains from the sky, the naked hills, the bed of the river covered by dry sand and many other details of my desert world. From the perspective of my childhood, with my humanity level with the ground, I knew, I know it to be dotted with scant vegetation, stony outcroppings, scattered bushes, and a deep ditch stained with vegetation, thanks to the subterranean water that at one time revealed itself in currents of water along those beds that now stretch out before my old man's curiosity. These were rivers that turned into mere whitish scars.

In that faraway time, when I was a child, I heard tell of the existence of trains that filled the rails with outrageous tooth marks to the rhythm of choo-choo and clackity-clack, clackity-clack. I heard about epileptic ships on mighty seas and about intertemporal airships. A lost pilgrim, I found joy in never before described panoramas. Upon hearing such fabulous portents I would fall into a pleasant drowsiness, overwhelmed by the onslaughts of a fantasy that ended up turning my poor imagination into a labyrinth inhabited by confusing voices and images.

Hold on a moment. . . . Yes . . . yes . . . yes, now I can see the line of hills, which look very flat from up here. Now I can make out the isolated huts as they appear. Over there's the cemetery, filled with crosses. That's where my loved ones are . . . where I . . . I try to make out the exact details. What happened to the roof that covered my childhood. Let's see, where was it, then, that I beheaded my first pigeon. The cactuses on whose flesh I carved my initials with the tip of a knife. On which hill? Where's the well that I fell into when the wind carried of my new hat, where they found me the next day at sunrise, asleep and clutching it.

Come on, Miguel, hurry up there, man, before this enormous airplane changes your landscape for a different one and leaves them behind in some sort of teary movie. No, there's no such thing as the future, only the advance of the past. Death doesn't approach; we go toward her. Get going, man!

I start a game I've invented on the spot without a shred of respect for the solemnity of Old Chronos.

From a distance of sixty-three years in time and a distance of thirty thousand feet high up in space, to the rhythm of a throbbing heart and an exterior beamlike flow, from these my places, which in this instant I make out from the mere heavens, I see myself as an eight-year-old child. To the side, a hut made from ocotillo branches, reeds, grass, mud, and a roof that turns green when it rains. I feel warm, intense tenderness. Desperate, I squint my eyes. I can't make out clearly the faces of the individuals with whom right now, yesterday I share, shared my infancy, right here on this spot of the world slipping away from me backwards with the speed at which this heartless machine is advancing. These topographies of God will never know shady forests.

But . . . damn, down there below, what's that I'm making out! I see a barefoot boy in rags. He's jumping up and down, lifting his arms, waving his hands. My God! It's me! I'm him!

He's waving hello to me! He's shouting and laughing like mad with joy. A big plane crosses overhead, one with a lot of windows. The incredible thing roars loudly, tracing a blurry tail of smoke.

I quickly forget the rules of the passing game. I excitedly return the greeting, waving my right hand and shouting: Byyye!

He disappears from me. I disappear from him.

I come to and settle back down, taken aback. I straighten my tie and adjust my glasses. I'm trembling, rubbing my tie pin, I draw my wrist up. . . . My watch has little diamonds instead of numbers. I cautiously look around me. In effect, a very pretty stewardess is standing next to me smiling.

Sir, you cried out just like a little boy.